Penguin Books

REVIVAL HOUSE

Julian Davies was born in 1954 in Melbourne. He now lives in the mountains near Canberra. This is his first novel.

REVIVAL HOUSE

JULIAN DAVIES

PENGUIN BOOKS

Penguin Books Australia Ltd
487 Maroondah Highway, PO Box 257
Ringwood, Victoria 3134, Australia
Penguin Books Ltd
Harmondsworth, Middlesex, England
Viking Penguin, A Division of Penguin Books USA Inc.
375 Hudson Street, New York, New York 10014, USA
Penguin Books Canada Limited
10 Aleorn Avenue, Toronto, Ontario, Canada M4Y 1E4
Penguin Books (N.Z.) Ltd
182-190 Wairau Road, Auckland 10, New Zealand

First published by Penguin Books Australia, 1991
10 9 8 7 6 5 4 3 2 1

Typeset in Australia by Midland Typesetters, Maryborough, Victoria.
Made and printed in Australia by Australian Print Group, Maryborough, Victoria.

National Library of Australia
Cataloguing-in-Publication data:

Davies, Julian, 1954-
Revival house.

ISBN 0 14 014624 5.

I. Title.

A823.3

Creative writing program assisted by the Literature Board of the Australian Council, the Federal Government's funding and advisory board.

To Kirb and Lloyd

Acknowledgement is gratefully made to the copyright holders of the following books, quotes from which have been used in *Revival House:*

Henry Clay Frick, The Man, George Harvey, Charles Scribner's Sons, 1928. Privately printed by the Frick Collection 1936.

Living My Life, Emma Goldman, Duckworth, London, 1930; Alfred Knopf, New York, 1931; Dover, New York, 1970.

Encyclopædia Britannica, 14th edition, copyright 1963 by Encyclopædia Britannica, Inc.

Duveen, S. N. Behrman, copyright 1950, 1951, 1952; Harmony Books, New York, 1982, by arrangement with Random House Inc.

Art Students' Anatomy, Edmond J. Farris, copyright 1935, 1944; J. B. Lippincott, 1935; Dover, New York, 1961.

Organized Labor in American History, Philip Taft, Harper and Row, New York, 1964.

Masterpieces of the Frick Collection, Introduction by Harry D. M. Grier, Frick Collection, New York, 1970.

The essential thing, to be sure, is that the workers also wear tuxedos or evening clothes. In other words: we want a kind of aristocratic Bolshevism.

Max Beckmann

I strenuously reject any suggestion that I am a breast fetishist. On the contrary, I feel I have a holistic approach to the female body.

Moishe Feinbaum

Speech is alive with the germ of commitment. The less you say, the less vulnerable you are.

S. N. Behrman

PART **ONE**

ONE
REPLAY

We were laughing. Moishe, head and bearded jaw tipped back, exposed his ample neck and Adam's apple. Steven's laughter shook his whole body.

'What can you say about Clarence? The man has an overdeveloped sense of duty to trivia. Unnecessary tasks occur to him compulsively. I met him one morning in the carpark. He'd walked all the way back to his car because he thought his seat belt was hanging out the door. Why worry, I asked. It might have gotten wet, he said. How? I looked about for a burst hydrant. It might rain, he replied.' Moishe, as usual, was lingering over his role as raconteur. 'Do I need to tell you the sky was blue and the seat belt was lying neatly on the car seat.

'Another time he agonised for over a week because he'd inadvertently ignored me in the corridor. When he finally mentioned it I couldn't even remember seeing him.'

'So, what did he do today?' asked Steven.

'The bastard has an uncanny ability to inflict pain on himself. He spilt yogurt on his office floor. He went down to the janitor's store to borrow a mop and found his wife – she's in the Special Science program – screwing some young student. God knows how, but within a couple of hours most of the college seemed to know about it.'

'Other people's adultery is entertainment.' Steven's tone suggested he was losing interest.

‘What do you expect? We enjoy a schlemiel and we enjoy sex. Clarence and his wife provide both.’

I did not recall this conversation until I had left Moishe Feinbaum’s house, left Island City and New York. In fact I didn’t remember it until I had been back in Australia several months. When I did recall it I relived it many times. It was like a scene from a movie, the significance of which has been missed until neatly clicking into place after the film is over, back home, over a cup of coffee, while rubbing tired eyes. But as a memory the scene could be replayed in several versions. Some of these versions were vividly distinct, still living as action in the present. Others were diffuse, hardly real.

Searching for clarity, I replayed the memory without words. Moishe, his lips moving, heavy forearms gesturing, was sprawled in his chair, thick thighs and calves thrust forward. A can of beer sat on the chair’s broad padded arm. Moishe’s shadow, cast in abstraction on the wall obliquely behind him, protruded in small mobile bumps from the compact shadow of his chair. Steven sat across from Moishe, his body angular, leaning forward, his shadow stretched along the floor. It was an elongated silhouette.

In another version of the scene I searched for a memory of myself. I was sitting at the third point of what was an undrawn equilateral triangle. I was silent. But did I have any real sense of having been in the room? Was my silence actually a sign of absence? I seemed to have observed the scene without having been there.

TWO
ARRIVAL

When I arrived in New York in late February 1982, Moishe met me at the airport. He was late.

'So, you're here,' he said, slapping me on the shoulders. I had been walking around the terminal for over half an hour looking for Moishe, and then had almost collided with him going out some electronic sliding doors at the main entrance. I recognised him immediately even though I hadn't seen him since I was six, except in the rare photograph he had remembered to send my parents. 'My God, but you look so young!' He took the suitcase out of my hand and shepherded me through the doorway. 'You could be one of my freshman students. Those kids get younger every year. I don't know what they've done to eighteen-year-olds to keep them so damned youthful; probably some hormone treatment. But I forget, you still *are* young!'

Moishe seemed in no hurry to find the car although it was raining heavily. I looked down at my feet soaked in a puddle I hadn't distinguished from the sheen of the carpark's wet asphalt.

'You'll come to love our weather,' commented Moishe. 'It's the only thing that reminds New Yorkers that nature and the universe are out there somewhere.' His voice was powerful, its American twang fresh to me although I had heard so many American voices in films.

Out on the road I peered expectantly through the car's front window for some sign of the city skyline. On the plane it had occurred to me that I probably knew as many of New York's street and place names as in my own home town, if not more. Broadway, Forty-second Street, Fifth Avenue, Park Avenue, Wall Street, Greenwich Village, Brooklyn Bridge, Times Square, Central Park, Harlem, the Bronx, Staten Island, Ellis Island, Long Island, Island City, even Yonkers had all repeated and crooned their way into my mental geography without the least knowledge of where, in fact, they were. Now I could see no sign of a real city. But that might, I thought, be due to the blur of rain and slapping windscreen wipers. What could be seen, a long stretch of bungalows and shops, seemed isolated by the night and storm.

'Seeing you and your suitcase reminded me of an airflight I took when I was eighteen. How old are you now?'

'Twenty-two.'

'So young! Anyhow, my parents sent me with my grandmother to England. It was the summer, a wonderful summer.' Unnervingly Moishe kept looking around at me while he drove. 'I was my Grandma's guide, or maybe guard would be a better definition of the role intended for me. Granny was a bit loopy. She had a thing for toilet brushes. After we took off she went to the restroom and was gone a long time. I found her up the back of the plane arguing with a steward. She was giving him a real hard time because there was no toilet brush in the restroom. I took her back to her seat. On the trip back here she brought her own. As soon as we were in the air she pulled the thing out of her carrybag. I tried to take it from her but she held it away from me, up in the air. I caught hold of her wrist just as a hostess was passing us. Remember I was eighteen and still capable of being embarrassed. I let go my grandmother's wrist and she got up and went down the aisle. I waited in my seat thinking about how incredibly clammy my palms were getting. The Fasten Seat Belt and No Smoking signs started flashing, members of the crew ran up and down the aisles. From the back of the plane I could hear shouting and pleading. You see, what my grandmother did with toilet brushes was to wrap paper around them and set them alight. By now I could smell burning plastic. Granny had locked herself in the bathroom and she stayed there until her task was complete. She remained buoyant for the rest of the flight despite aggressive questioning from the crew. Burning toilet brushes was like a spiritual mission for my grandmother.'

That night I saw nothing of the city I had expected to find, but Moishe gave me a sort of corollary. It later occurred to me that there could be few places more suited to the natural evolution of stories, of anecdotes and myths than New York. At times I wondered if it were possible to live there without memory slipping into anecdote and anecdote memory; and without memory's events recurring as part of a continuous present. I had an occasional fantasy that all the movies ever set in Manhattan might come alive on the streets in one grand and chaotic enactment of the city's labyrinthine mythology.

We pulled into the kerb. Moishe had something to buy at a drugstore. Drugstore; the term, although foreign to Australia, was familiar enough. But now, neon lettering in icy blue was tangible evidence that I had left the uniform limbo of long-distance air travel. I wound down the window to see this new reality more clearly. The rain pricked at my face and a man looked down at me as he passed leaning into the wind. He was wearing a red and black checked lumber-jacket, which was ripped open across his back. Long greying hair curled out at his collar. Even as I smiled automatically I realised he was looking through me.

'Here we are,' said Moishe. 'Your first glimpse of your new home!'

We turned into the driveway of a wooden house, painted white and overshadowed by windblown pine trees.

THREE
FAMILY ALBUM

'Do you want to see my album?'

I was sitting on my bed in my room in the basement. From the bed I could see the furnace, its black pipes reaching around the next room. Ruth, the Feinbaum's second child, was standing at my door. She was twelve years old.

'Yes, I'd like that. What is it, photos?'

'Yes, and no.'

She walked over to the bed and sat beside me, placing the book on her knees so that the cover opened onto mine.

The first page was filled by an enlargement, probably a school photograph, of Ruth with pigtails and blue ribbons, aged about eight. She had an expression of intensely brazen confidence.

'This is me, when I was young. And this,' she said, turning the page, 'is my family.' For a second I was disconcerted. The family was there, on the left page, but had been reinvented and adorned. Elizabeth, Ruth's mother, stood at the centre – but her thighs, in shorts, were those of a muscular black man. Her left arm, her own to the elbow, was transformed thereafter, a hairy forearm projecting at right angles to her body and holding a basketball in its massive hand. Her hair, usually short and black, had been remade long and golden and was covered with flowers. The flowers had been cut from a photograph double the scale of Elizabeth's head and gave her an aura of tropical fecundity.

Ruth began to turn the page.

'Wait, this is interesting, I'd like to look at it longer.'

She glanced at me and smiled.

'Did you take the photos yourself?'

'My sister takes them and gives me the ones she doesn't want.'

'And all these extra things, did you cut them from magazines?'

'Yes, and catalogues.'

'How do you choose them?' I was looking at Hannah, Ruth's sister, who was at the left edge of the group. She was attractive although her head sat on the standing body of a man wearing a pin-stripe suit, one leg crossed in front of the other. Hannah, who was fifteen, had kept her rich, brown, shoulder-length hair except for a baseball cap which seemed to hover a little above her head. Her own hands held a camera in front of her chest.

'They just look right.'

Moishe was turned towards Hannah. It was a full length picture of him in tee-shirt and shorts. He was unchanged but for an uncomfortable reworking of his arms, one of which had a golf bag tucked under it, while the other held up a baseball bat. In the foreground, cutting off Elizabeth's knees, was a Volkswagen beetle on the scale of a large family dog. The Feinbaum's second car was just such a Volkswagen. Herman, Ruth's eight-year-old brother, had been placed in the car, his head poking through a hole in the roof. He was grinning broadly. Ruth's own head had been transplanted onto the body of a tanned young woman wearing a bikini. Her youthfully curled, dark hair had been stuck arbitrarily to the woman's shoulders. She stood, hands on hips at the right of the group, garlands of gorgeous flowers at her feet.

On the opposite page was a freehand drawing. It was an outline of the family group, the figures featureless and shimmering in a blue and yellow fluorescent light.

There was a loud clatter on the stairs and Hannah and Herman, followed by their father, entered the room.

'We're having a pool play-off, do you guys want to join in?'

Moishe was loud and his tone all-embracing. A pool table filled nearly half of my room. It was not all that unusual for me to be in bed at night reading while Ruth and Herman shouted at each other over a pool game. Herman had a habit of hitting the cue ball so hard that it flew off the table. It often shot under my bed where Herman then crawled in search.

'We're busy,' said Ruth. She turned the page. Here there was a series of unaltered photographs of all three children at various ages.

'Ah, the family history.' Moishe had come across and was looking over my shoulder. 'Just look at this,' he said; 'you make children and then set off an inescapable chain reaction, a process of ceaseless cell division, until these new people are as big as you are. Or, with postwar protein, even bigger. You'd expect each generation would get slightly smaller as a mark of respect, of filial duty to its parents. Isn't that so kids?'

'Yeah, great idea, Dad,' said Hannah, turning her back on him.

'Pygmy people, pygmy people!' Ruth had shut her book, got up and was jumping about.

'But everyone would disappear,' said Herman, dismayed.

FOUR
GEOGRAPHY

When I caught a bus, after returning to Australia, I almost inevitably thought of riding by bus at night from Brooklyn to Island City. And then I would think of Moishe. The connection between these things may seem arbitrary but for me it was persistent. There was a bus, any bus, there was a specific New York bus trip, and then there was Moishe. After that I was drawn back, caught by those episodes the mind chooses to retain from everything lived. I finally decided to try to make sense of these memories. There seemed to be a pattern in the experience that could only be decoded by the structure of writing it out. So I started the project and was immediately surprised by how fleeting my material seemed to be.

At the time Ruth first showed me her album I had been living with the Feinbaums for about a month. When reconstructing this scene I spent a disproportionate amount of time on Moishe, when he was looking over my shoulder and commenting on 'the family history'. Did he actually say 'a process of ceaseless cell division'? Might he have said instead, 'a process of growth', or merely 'children grow up'? How much of my later attitude to Moishe, my compounded – or is it *scattered* – knowledge of him, alters my memory? How much does the personality Moishe wished to project become self-perpetuating? I had only my subjective ear. Of course, Moishe would not have said 'children grow up'. This lacks his normal tone and flourish. But there were many more subtle questions than this.

I also had trouble reconstructing myself newly arrived in the Feinbaums' household. I was so different then.

'It's a forty-minute drive to Manhattan,' said Elizabeth.

'Ah, that explains why I couldn't see anything of the city last night.'

It was the morning after my arrival. Elizabeth had sat me at the table with Moishe and was serving us breakfast. In the morning light Moishe seemed larger, hairier as he ate his fried eggs with relaxed speed and promised to drive me to the city soon. In the meantime I could see the skyline from the edge of the bay.

I walked the block and a half to the bay, more aware of my own breath, white on the air, than my surroundings. I had never experienced such cold. I hurried across Bayside Drive, the main commuter road for all of Island City, taking advantage of a brief gap in the traffic, and rested against the chest-high concrete wall bordering the water.

The view beyond the wall was a highly obtuse meeting of abstract planes. Or so it seemed to my eyes used to a coastline of varied and insistent physical reality. The bay, unmarked by any sign of shipping, was a wide band of dull grey. Brooklyn, a narrower strip of mottled and paler grey, arched at a low angle above the bay. There were buildings at the edge of the water, featureless in the distance. Beyond Brooklyn and thrown up against the horizon were the cardboard cutout skyscrapers of downtown and midtown Manhattan. So, this was it. I recalled how, as a nine or ten-year-old, I had discussed with my friends the tallest building in the world, how it swung in the wind and how a coin dropped from its top would embed itself so many metres into the pavement. To those boys the

Empire State Building, many thousands of kilometres away, had symbolised the alluring dangers of extremity. I could see it now, even in this abstracted form, standing out among the greys of midtown. I leant against the wall waiting for something to break the spell of unreality, for a boat to cut apart the flat grey of the bay or an aeroplane to give dimension to the faint blue backdrop of sky.

The geography of New York only became absolutely real for me nearly two years later, as I was leaving. I had a window seat on an aeroplane with a flight path which skirted the Atlantic coast and I looked down over the whole city, made three-dimensional by my rapid elevation from its flat expanse. As I left it behind, Manhattan's true mass rose up in gravity-defying clusters. The spectacle seemed to mirror the massive void opening out inside me as I was carried away. And so my attention was drawn almost directly below me to where I could see the full length of Island City. Seen in its entirety for the first time it reminded me of a leg and club foot viewed from the side. I could clearly see the avenues running the full length of the leg and dividing it into four narrow blocks of houses laid out in grid pattern between the bay and the Atlantic. The scene of the previous twenty months of my life was encapsulated in a pattern of small rectangles. The iron girders of the Bay Park Bridge, connecting the Island with Brooklyn, were now a tidy arrangement of grey match-sticks. I hurriedly searched for the Feinbaums' house and found it, found the dark dots of its pine trees.

I walked back to the house. The three pines were the tallest trees in the street. The night before, they had overshadowed the house, black, shifting, undefined. Today they were a fresh green, standing elegantly to the left of the steps leading to the front door. The Feinbaums, it was clear, were not gardeners. The front lawn was matted with fallen pine needles and there were no garden beds. By contrast all the neighbouring houses had tidy lawns and neat azalea hedges. Later I learnt that no one in Island City gardened. Trucks pulled up on appointed days, the grass was cut, the plants pruned and fallen leaves blown into the street by noisy machines that performed the reverse role of vacuum cleaners. But the Feinbaums did not observe even this custom.

I remember Moishe talking about gardening, once. He had mentioned the unlikely marriage of Australians in suburbia to the quarter-acre block with its vegetable garden and flower beds. And the cult of the weekend lawn mowing. Incredible!

'Elizabeth's parents are gardeners, but they live in the country.' He made it sound like another country. 'They grow everything you'd ever wish to eat, to see, to experience. Even in their bathroom there are hanging plants. You have to be wary brushing your teeth, or you get a fern frond in the eye. I had a dream once that I was eating with them and had to pull weeds out of my place-mat. Gardeners are forever weeding.'

When I remembered the Feinbaums' house later I most frequently pictured it from the street, sliced open in cross-section, like a doll's house. I looked into every room as though there were windows in the internal walls. The children's rooms were all on the top floor, opening onto the landing. Hannah's room was uncluttered, with the determination of a teenage fad. Everything was grey. Her desk was tidy, her bed was a futon on a wooden platform. On the walls were neatly pinned rows of photographs she had taken. Clothes hung out from a full basket. In Ruth's room there were posters on the walls of rock bands whose members were all women. There was a complete drum kit by the bed and an acoustic guitar against one wall. The walls were still papered with a pattern of pink elephants wearing hats, and stuffed animals and dolls lined two long shelves. Herman's room was chaotic. Nothing was visible because everything was under something else. There were posters of various bats, hanging upside down or with wings spread. Indeed, the room had a slight smell suggestive of a cave occupied by bats. Two fish, one missing an eye, circled in a semi-stagnant bowl. But where were the children? Looking down into the house I searched for the family. Moishe and Elizabeth's room was empty, so was the bathroom. Downstairs the living-room, dining-room and kitchen were are all deserted. So too was the basement. Everyone was out.

FIVE
WARBURGS

We were driving down Bayside Drive. I was in the back seat with Ruth and Hannah. Elizabeth was driving and Moishe had Herman on his knee. Before we left the house Moishe had told me that his masculinity was not in such jeopardy that he needed to assert it behind a steering wheel. 'Besides which,' he had added, 'Elizabeth is a nervous passenger.'

We were on our way to Warburgs which, I had been told, was the local supermarket. Everyone had come for the ride, perhaps lured by the promise of ice-cream after the shopping. There were roadworks ahead and we slowed down.

'They're digging up the street again.' Herman was at that age where commentary on the obvious was irresistable. I had been there for less than a week and already he had read to me from numerous advertising signs.

'Again?' I asked automatically.

'This is the second time this year, and last year it was pulled up two or three times.' Elizabeth sounded matter-of-fact but she looked earnest, sitting close to the wheel. As we passed the excavation, I noticed it was alarmingly deep.

'Can we get Oreos?' pleaded Ruth.

'What are "Oreos"?'

'You don't know what Oreos are?' Herman had turned around and was staring at me over his father's shoulder.

'What do you eat in Australia!' For Ruth I had dropped way beneath contempt. Hannah, I noticed, sat quietly, looking ahead, ignoring the noise around her. Her camera lay in her lap.

We turned into a carpark and I saw the shabby brick facade of the supermarket. The centre of the parking area was sunken, and that day, after earlier rain, formed a huge puddle at least ten metres across. As we left the car Moishe clasped my arm and pointed to the water.

'We call this Lake Warburgs.'

The shopping carts, lined up in front of the supermarket entrance, were jammed up together. Moishe and I tugged at several, unsuccessfully. A small woman in a fur coat stood watching us critically.

'You're doing it all wrong,' she said. 'You have to pull at an angle.'

'Look lady, do you want to do it?' Moishe, I discovered, was capable of a tone of authoritative disdain.

'I was only trying to be helpful.'

Inside, Moishe was led away by the children in search of what he called 'television necessities'. Elizabeth had asked me to help her with the 'regular' shopping.

'Do you have supermarkets like this in Australia?'

'Something like it.' After the scene outside, in fact after five days of being made aware of my every peculiarity, I was not at all sure of any commonality. In any case, I had had little to do with supermarkets, living with parents who had done most of the shopping.

'Would you get me two boxes of matzohs? They're in the next aisle.'

'I beg your pardon?'

'Matzohs. You don't know what matzohs are? It's unleavened bread – crackers.'

I walked along the aisle looking for this unknown substance. Halfway along there was a large amber pool with black wheel tracks from the shopping carts criss-crossing in a tight network on each side. Someone had knocked over a bottle of apple cider. I picked my way around the puddle and glass shards, looking amongst the array of biscuit packages. I reached the end of the aisle without success and retraced my steps worrying that I would have to bare my foreign accent by asking advice.

When, matzohs in hand, I found Elizabeth she had the cart half-full.

Moishe and the children passed us. Herman, riding on the cart, held up a box to me.

'See – Oreos!' Then they were gone, down another aisle.

While we all waited in queue Moishe explained to me the mystery of 'television necessities'.

'There are two distinct classes within the larger family. The first category consists of those products essential for comfortable television viewing. This requires personal discrimination and I'm all in favour of it.' He pointed out several items in the shopping cart: beer, smoked oysters and dill pickles. 'The other category involves me in a constant war of attrition with the children. These products are made necessary by television advertising. They involve no judgement, only brainwashing. Every new shampoo, cookie or TV meal becomes the subject of intense bargaining for a place on the shopping list. I like to make the kids fight for them, invent justifications for their unbridled consumerism.' He showed me a box of breakfast cereal, illustrated on the front by brightly coloured cartoon characters. 'These things are filled with marshmallow and covered with sugar and chocolate. And they eat this junk at 7.00am on an empty stomach.'

On the way home we all licked at ice-cream cones: chocolate

chip, butter pecan, peanut cookie crunch, rum raisin, fudge ripple. Ruth's agile tongue forced the ice-cream down into the cone; Elizabeth concentrated on staunching the drips, while steering with one hand; Hannah toyed with hers, licking it up into a delicate peak; Moishe's massive tongue demolished his in what seemed to be several swipes; Herman's ice-cream dropped off the cone onto his lap.

SIX
DEMOGRAPHY

One of the first conversations I had with Moishe was demographic. My parents tell me I was about six at the time. The story is a typical family anecdote. It has been repeated often enough that I am no longer certain I don't vaguely recall it myself. Moishe and I were travelling on a bus together in the centre of Sydney, on our way home. The rush-hour crowd filled the streets. Watching the hurrying people I remarked to Moishe what a large number there seemed to be.

'About two and a half million in the whole city,' Moishe stated.

'Two and a half million people?'

'Yes.'

'Does that include us?'

When I mentioned this episode to Moishe in New York he had no memory of it.

Moishe had arrived in Australia when I was five, attracted by the chance to work as a graduate student with my father. He and my father became friends, and eventually Moishe moved into our spare room for the second year of his stay.

During my time in New York Moishe quite frequently became nostalgic about his Australian experience.

'You know, when I went to my professor and told him I wanted to do my Ph.D. on urban populations in Australia he looked at me like I was off my brain.

' "What, populations of kangaroos?" The man thought he had a sense of humour. I told him your country is one of the most urbanised on earth. At that time, I think, about two-thirds of the people lived in the big cities. My family thought I was stepping off the edge of the planet. At the airport, my Aunt Esther gave me a canvas water-bottle for fear I'd die of thirst. I had to go into the men's room and empty it out.

'I've never regretted the decision. Your parents were good to me. You could stay with us for the rest of your life and invite in several friends and I wouldn't have repaid the debt.'

Elizabeth, who had walked into the living-room while Moishe was talking, paused and looked at me.

'The only thing he ever gets at all sentimental about is your family. The anniversary of his arrival in Australia is more important than all our birthdays and anniversaries put together. He's only once ever brought me flowers – a bunch of red roses the second time we went out together.'

'There were two dozen roses.' Moishe didn't seem at all perturbed by this assault. 'And they weren't red, they were crimson. And you know, my liebeh, this is inaccurate, I brought you flowers another time.'

'When?'

'When Hannah was born.'

'Oh yes, how could I forget.' Elizabeth turned back to me. 'He arrived late, just after Hannah was born. The nurse held the baby up for Moishe to see and he got very upset. You know how loud his voice gets. He wanted to know what had been done to his daughter. Hannah was born with an unusually thick, white layer of protective oil on her skin.'

'OK, laugh at me, but the kid looked like someone had smeared her with cream cheese. How was I to know? It looked very worrying. I checked it out in the encyclopædia when I got home. The *vernix caseosa* it's called, and it sounded pretty unpleasant. It's some sort of gross mixture of dead cells, salt, fat, cholesterol and God knows what else. Wouldn't you be worried? The *vernix caseosa*! Hannah was always a different child, even at birth.'

The decision to study in Australia had not harmed Moishe's career. His work had been so highly regarded that at the time of my arrival in New York he was head of his department at Island City College, at the age of forty.

Moishe's sentimentality for my parents interested me when I started trying to make sense of my own time as a part of his family. With a conservative Jewish background Moishe entered our atheistic, politically radical household. Both my parents had vigorous intellects; my mother was a political scientist and my father, of course, a demographer. In the relative clarity of their way of life I suppose they were eccentric. We owned no car, television, dish-washer or power lawn-mower. This was not so much a conscious decision as a simple act of omission. The idolatory of the consumable object had little influence in their lives. I think this had some sort of attraction for Moishe. We were also, and I know he enjoyed this, a very close family. One of my school friends, whose parents were political activists associated with my mother and father, attempted suicide at the age of fifteen. I remember him telling me that he felt absolutely alone. At his house I used to sense an atmosphere of almost complete alienation from the practice of daily living. This depressed me. In retrospect I am impressed at the ease with which my parents seemed to combine their intellectual life with the rhythms of a generously run household. We always ate well, together at the table, no matter what else was happening.

'The conversation! I found the definition of civilisation where I least expected it: at a family dinner table in Sydney, Australia in 1965. My family could talk, God they could talk, but every night I sat down with your parents to a feast of conversation.' I never saw Moishe more genuinely enthusiastic.

Moishe was fun. That is how I remember him when I was five or six.

'It amuses me that I can remember you as a small kid,' Moishe told me while we sat together in the living-room one evening. 'You used to hang around like Herman does now. You had some Anglo-Saxon restraint, but you could still pester.'

Moishe and my parents kept in contact, if somewhat haphazardly, through the years. It was my father who suggested I apply for a graduate place at Island City College. My field, Art History, had a good reputation there. And life in America would be a different experience for me. As usual my father was right. With my family's influence it was the social and political aspects of art that particularly interested me. The 'New York School', the painters of the 1940s and '50s, was my proposed area of study. The arrival of this art movement signalled New York's emergence as the international art capital at the same time the United States achieved worldwide political and economic dominance. It was this connection that I intended to research. I planned that my work would achieve results that would launch a career for me as an academic.

SEVEN
AMERICAN SHABBES

Elizabeth was saying a prayer, in Hebrew. I was fascinated by the sudden transformation of her voice. Earlier this day I had watched her make bread called 'challah'. The first syllable of challah, she had stressed, should be a gutteral *ha*. Throughout this explanation and the rest of our conversation her voice had remained a fleshing out of the disembodied voices of American women I had seen in movies. This had been interesting enough, connecting an American accent with the mobility and expression of a face at last freed from Hollywood dialogue. But now, without warning, she was making exotic and musical sounds. She sat opposite me, her face made soft by candlelight. I looked around to see Moishe watching me from the head of the table, smiling. I was used to the ordered clutter of my own family dinner table yet here I was an initiate. Hannah, now, was saying a prayer, in English. I felt a little awkward, not because I was uncomfortable but, perversely, because I feared the Feinbaums were worrying that I was uncomfortable. I raised my glass and drank a moment behind the family. Another prayer was said, by Ruth, hurriedly, as though to get it over with. Elizabeth broke the challah and gave us each a piece, which we all ate.

'So,' said Moishe, clapping the table with the flat of his palms. 'Now you are a Jew!' We all laughed.

This was my first Friday evening in New York, the beginning of my first Shabbes, or Sabbath, meal. Even the movies had failed to prepare me for the strength of Jewish culture in New York. The self-depreciation of Jewish humour had outwitted me. I hadn't sensed that it was a symptom of an ubiquitous presence. I didn't know, for instance, that nearly everyone in New York eats bagels. In fact, I doubt I had ever heard the word *bagel*. I discovered that 'blintzes' and 'knishes' were foods as fast as hotdogs and hamburgers. Out walking I would pass a temple every few blocks and sometimes pause to listen to the sound of chanting just audible through the walls.

Earlier that Friday, while I watched Elizabeth kneading the dough for the challah, Herman came into the kitchen. He went to one of the drawers and took out a loaf of bread packaged in bright red and yellow plastic. From another drawer he took a knife and, from a cupboard, a jar. All this he brought to the kitchen table, and sat down beside me. By this time his mother had rolled the dough out into three long strips. She joined them at one end and began to braid them together. Herman took out two slices of bread so white I wondered about its ingredients. He then opened the jar. Its contents looked like peanut butter, but peanut butter shot through with fat veins of clear purple mucous.

'What's that?'

'Goobergrape.' He was concentrating on spreading thick smears, marbled like dripping and blood, on his bread.

' "Goobergrape"?'

'Yep, Goobergrape. Want some?'

'No thanks. Is the purple stuff grape jam?'

'Grape jelly.' He corrected me with the authority of an adult.

'We call it jam.'

He shrugged.

Elizabeth completed her braiding. She then painted the top of the bread with egg white and sprinkled it with poppy seeds. Herman got up from the table and was halfway out the door with his sandwich before his mother called him back.

'Put away your stuff, Herman.' She took up the bread pan as she spoke and slipped it into the oven.

So, this was my first Sabbath, my first American Sabbath. Elizabeth was carving roast chicken. Moishe filled my wine glass. The children began to talk as they passed the bowl of mashed potatoes, the cranberry jelly, and the golden twisted challah.

'Do you realise this is a bird that we're eating?' said Ruth, shaking out her dark curls.

'Chickens can't fly,' retorted Hannah. 'As far as I'm concerned if you can't fly you're not a bird.'

'Marny Weisman owns an Amazonian parrot.' Herman looked around at everyone as he spoke.

'Pass the dressing, please Dad,' said Hannah.

'He can copy everyone in the family's voice. And he likes to talk to you. If people don't talk to him he pulls out his own feathers.'

'That's a remedy for loneliness I haven't yet tried,' said Moishe.

'When are you ever lonely?' demanded Elizabeth.

'Would any of you eat a parrot? I mean, if there was nothing else.' After nearly a week I was beginning to understand that questions like this were typical of Ruth's conversational technique. 'There's just you and this parrot left together in a locked room. And you're both getting hungry. And it's a big parrot.' Ruth glanced at Hannah as she spoke. Before this I had noticed Ruth seeking her elder sister's attention. At times she talked more and more quickly, recklessly, as though determined to win her approval. Hannah seemed to be concentrating on her food.

'Ruth, you're scaring Herman,' warned Elizabeth. Indeed, Herman looked small and pale.

'Next you'll put us on a desert island with only a week's supply of water, a box of matches, the abridged edition of *War and Peace* and a parrot. What would you do? will be the question.'

'That's a great idea, Dad. What would you do?' persisted Ruth.

'I'd make pretty sure I kept talking. I don't fancy being left on an island with a naked parrot.'

'No, seriously, if you had to live for the rest of your life on an island and you could take only five different things to eat, what would you take?'

'I'd take beer, I'd take bagels, cream cheese and lox, and I'd take dill pickles.'

'I'd take chocolate, pizza, hot dogs, hamburgers and ice-cream.' Herman was cheered up.

'I only need two things,' said Ruth, 'chocolate and ice-cream.'

EIGHT
NINETEENTH-CENTURY AMERICAN DREAM

It was Elizabeth who first took me to Manhattan, on the second day after my arrival.

'I want to get you to the city while you're still fresh and impressionable. Usually I drive but I think we should take the subway so you come up in Manhattan totally unprepared.'

'Thanks for preparing me.'

In fact, I wasn't prepared even for the subway. You would think I hadn't grown up in a city. In the station, standing beside Elizabeth waiting for the train, I looked down at the track. Dark water was flowing around the rails. A cardboard Coca Cola cup glided past and then a sodden piece of paper trailed by, its submerged half dragging against the sleepers. It was incongruous, the speed of this stream deep underground, flowing around the train track. Where was it going? Then there was the smell that became inseparable from any memory of the subway. It was a smell with many subtle variations; winter and summer, station to station. At its heart were the constant odours of grinding metal and stale urine, carried on wafts of hot air.

I clearly remember our arrival in the city, despite the overlay of many later visits. It was an extremely cold day. My face felt the sting of the air as we came up from the close atmosphere of the subway. Elizabeth brought me out in Chinatown on Canal Street. My immediate impression of the street was not of its ethnic character but of its architecture. I had expected to come up among skyscrapers. Instead the buildings were squat. Consequently the street seemed wide and the sky surprisingly broad. External metal fire-escapes formed delicate abstract patterns against the sides of buildings. My disorientation was augmented by steam, thick and white, rising from subway vents in the sidewalk and billowing from pipes opening out of the walls and roofs of buildings. This might have been a site of volcanic activity. I briefly imagined that the layered seams of bitumen in the street described the curvature of the earth, and that the crust and mantle had dissolved leaving a thin layer of human construction floating on a molten core. The concrete under my feet shuddered as a train passed beneath us.

Elizabeth caught my hand for a moment, to start me moving up the street. The sidewalk was crowded with people wrapped up in winter clothing. Benches were set up in front of the shops, arrayed with fresh vegetables. We passed several stands covered with fish, their sleek black and silver bodies laid out between crushed ice. A man wielding a large rectangular cleaver yelled out loudly in Chinese to someone in a passing van. Plucked chickens hung by their necks behind several shop windows.

We lunched at a dumpling house. The place was nearly empty so we sat at a table for four, taking an extra chair each for our coats, scarves, gloves and woollen hats. A waitress busied herself around us placing heavy white china, which was still hot and moist from being washed. I thanked her.

'Welcomes,' she replied.

Each time either of us thanked her, as she brought in turn hot Chinese tea, hot and sour soup, and fried dumplings, she repeated this variation on the usual expression. We became more polite than was necessary in order to hear her reply. Already I was aware of feeling comfortable with Elizabeth. And Moishe? With Moishe, I realised, I had begun to feel like a welcome spectator at an intimate performance.

'I really appreciate you spending your day off as my tour guide.'

'What else would I be doing? Shopping at Warburgs or mopping the kitchen floor.'

'You work four days a week?'

'Three.'

'That sounds like a nice balance.'

'I only work because Moishe wants me to. He says we need the money. It's OK. The realtor I work for is a rude man but I'm out of the office most of the day. The clients are entertaining – so many of them are whacky.'

'Whacky?'

'The number of men who think a prearranged appointment to appraise their house is an invitation for unusual sexual practices, you wouldn't believe.'

'What do you do?'

'Do you mean what sort of unusual practices?' She laughed. 'I see you embarrass easily. No, if they're persistent I leave.'

'Obviously it doesn't worry you?'

'I have a working theory that anything is possible, that there is no such thing as middle-class normality.'

'What about violence?'

'I've only met one case of threatened violence. A client was released from a mental hospital to close the sale of the family house. I arrived at the appointed time to find a bonfire burning in the front yard and his wife hiding behind her car. He'd piled up all the living-room furniture and set fire to it. His wife warned me he was hiding upstairs with a shotgun.' Elizabeth sat back in her chair, smiling.

'What happened?'

'Oh, the police arrived and arrested him without a struggle. But the sale of the house fell through.'

'Yes?'

'You're surprised? The buyers were a married couple and the woman didn't work. She was worried that the former owner might drop in while her husband was away during the day.'

I found myself listening to Elizabeth for what distinguished her as an American woman. There seemed to be a quality I couldn't identify which was independent of accent, turn of phrase or of any other obvious characteristic. This quality dazzled me with its intangibility. It both attracted and disquieted me.

'So, what would you like to do after lunch?'

'I'd like to leave it up to you.'

'Alright, we won't sightsee. We'll take a taxi uptown to the Frick Collection.'

'Why the Frick Collection?'

'I know it's not your particular area, but it is an art museum, and it's my favorite. I'd like to be the first to take you there.'

That was how it happened. Elizabeth introduced me to the Frick. I remember the mood of detached enjoyment of that first visit. Elizabeth was more interested in the atmosphere of the place than in looking at any particular painting for long.

She revelled in the exotic domestic setting of a collection of European art which, although quite small, was, I realised, of unusual quality. Before leaving we sat on one of the stone benches in the central courtyard. Dark-leafed plants stood completely still, caught in opaque light from the clouded glass of the roof high above. Water fell lightly from the fountain in the long pool in the middle of the courtyard, as though gravity were held back from this place slightly. Indeed, the mundane influence of material reality seemed to be waived here before some more eccentric force. I was entranced by the quaintness of Frick's legacy. Here was a nineteenth century American dream of a Baroque villa existing tranquilly in a twentieth century metropolis.

'Do you know anything about Frick?'

'He made his money from steel, at least I think that was it.'

'One of those millionaires of America's industrialisation. Did he actually live here?'

'Only for the last few years of his life.'

I thought about the luxurious rooms behind us, still decorated and furnished as the dead man's house. They were filled with his pictures, the ones he bought and brought across the Atlantic. They were now available to anyone walking on Seventieth Street and willing to pay one dollar for admittance. But how had they been acquired?

'I vaguely recall reading something about Frick. Wasn't he Carnegie's strong man and something of a strike-breaker?'

'Andrew Carnegie? I really don't know.'

NINE
PHOTOGRAPHY

We were on the beach, Hannah, Ruth, Herman and I. Hannah was taking photographs. She lined all of us up against the background of ocean and sky and took our group portrait. The polaroid camera snapped and whirred like one of Herman's electric cars, and the photo popped out the bottom.

'Can I hold it,' pleaded Herman.

'Don't get sand on it or I'll kill you.'

Hannah constantly took photographs. Her parents gave her a film allowance and she babysat two nights a week to earn enough money to support her camera.

'We're starting to come out,' said Herman excitedly. No matter how many photographs he saw develop, Herman was fascinated, when he was in them. I looked over him. Sure enough we were emerging in the padding of our thick coats. The horizon line neatly ran behind my waist, Ruth's chest and Herman's shoulders.

'I don't look like that.' Ruth was adamant.

'Of course you do.' Hannah sounded defensive, as though her ability as a photographer had been slighted.

'No I don't, but Herman is cute.'

'Herman's always cute, he's just too cute.'

Herman looked as though he knew how cute he was, and that was, as Hannah said, just too cute. I marvelled at what seemed to me to be an essential Americanism and decided to look up *cute* in the Feinbaums' Webster's version of the dictionary, and in my own Oxford and Macquarie versions. When I was growing up, *cute* was not part of my family's vocabulary; sweet, charming, delightful, even precious but never cute.

'He's the cutest!' Ruth moved to tickle her brother and they ran off down the beach, Herman squealing loudly.

The beach was low and flat and the houses were only thirty metres from the water's edge. I could easily imagine a storm throwing waves into the streets, and said so to Hannah.

'I think it happened once or twice, but not for a long time.'

I wondered what would be her definition of a long time as I watched her aiming her camera at a jogger wearing a tracksuit, blue with white racing stripes. He passed us at the water's edge with the heavy thud of feet on wet sand. He looked at Hannah, aggrieved as the camera clacked. She turned away with the detached poise of a professional. Ruth and Herman were small in the distance, still scuttling around. The beach stretched away, undistinguished but for regularly spaced rows of decaying wood pylons, jetties built in the 1960s to stop sand erosion. They diminished like a basic exercise in perspective drawing. By contrast the buildings on the edge of the beach, houses in the foreground and increasingly larger apartment blocks in the distance, seemed to reverse accepted laws. I looked from jetties to buildings intrigued by the conflict between perception and reality.

'Dad is always telling me that photography is a craft not an art. What do you think about that?'

'It's only one idea; what do you think yourself?' I was slightly taken aback, by the nature of the question and because this was really the first time, after nearly a month, that Hannah had initiated conversation with me.

'I asked you first.'

'Some people say it's the decision about where to point the camera and when to press the button, the quality of the creative instant, that determines whether a photograph is a work of art or not.'

'Some people say, but what do you say?'

'I don't suppose I have a really strong opinion. Perhaps there are as many possible answers as there are good photographers. Anyway, I like looking at photos.'

'Me too, especially photos of people. You can stare at them without being rude.'

'I hadn't thought of it quite like that.'

'It's the same with movies, you can watch people that way too. But that's not all.'

'No?'

'Forget the stories in movies. The stars are real people. They're playing parts but you're watching real people doing real things. And often they're doing things you don't get to see in real life. You see what I mean?'

'I think so.'

'Someone might ask me what I think of some movie but often I don't care. I've been looking at the people and haven't listened to the story.'

We walked along in silence, watching our feet scuffing the sand. I was surprised by this conversation, not least because Hannah led me through it. I looked up to see Ruth running back towards us.

'Hannah! Herman dropped the photo!'

Hannah was immediately transformed by the need for sisterly vengeance. Both girls chased their brother, who ran away desperately. I watched until they caught him, knocked him over into the sand and started pinching and tickling. I then turned to look out to sea. A couple of large tankers were visible near the horizon line. The ocean was a cold lustreless grey, and the waves dumped in small compact curls as though impatient to break apart.

TEN
CHUTZPAH

Island City College was in fact in Brooklyn. The campus sat up against the approaches to the Bay Park Bridge and was oriented to face the bay. On clear days, looking out from the upper storey of the Art History Department, I could see the dark smudge of the Feinbaums' pine trees, an isolated dab of deep green beyond the water.

I drove with Moishe to the college the morning after my first trip into the city. We took the Volkswagen, both of us sitting in the front, the radio on, the windows shut tight. The de-mister and our breath vied for control of the windscreen. I looked up at the roof half expecting signs of an opening, half expecting Ruth's reordered photographs to have affected reality also. Moishe talked above the radio, explaining the layout of the college and the steps of my registration. My attention was intercepted by snatches of the morning news, by its style more than its content. One news item, I remember, was relayed from an Alaskan sister station called 'King Jesus at the North Pole'.

Moishe became quiet, apparently listening to the radio. I began to think about the previous afternoon at the Frick Collection. There was something about the place which basically interested me. Or was it the inspiration behind it? There seemed to be an historical quirk at work here. What sort of person had collected those rare things and placed them in a setting as perfectly conceived as it was anachronistic? I pictured the diffuse light and softly falling water of the central courtyard. Of course, Frick wasn't unique in his period. I recalled a story about Andrew Mellon, another millionaire of America's industrialisation and the founder of the National Gallery in Washington. He had bought a Titian Venus which he wouldn't hang in his house because of the female flesh it displayed. He wouldn't hang religious paintings where his friends might smoke or drink. These sort of values reflected culture grafted onto a society just beginning to assert its power.

I was pretty sure Frick had been a pre-eminently practical man and uncompromising in business. But he had obviously turned a great part of his wealth to the collection of art and to building its extraordinary setting. Wasn't there a connection here with the period I was about to begin studying? That first truly powerful generation with its earnest determination to import civilisation might be the precursor of the ascendant generation which spawned an indigenous school of painting. This could prove interesting.

But what really surprised me was the quality of the things Frick had bought.

Moishe parked the car and we climbed up onto a broad paved square bounded on three sides by buildings. Several dozen people, spread out across the square and crossing it in different directions, seemed small, dwarfed by the scale of their surroundings. There was an oppressive background noise, a mechanical roaring, but no one, including Moishe, showed any sign of concern. As we approached the centre of the square the noise became louder. On drawing close I could see down into a deeply sunken central courtyard, at the bottom of which was a grimy blue machine on wheels. Although only about the size of a small car it was the source of the roaring. Several cables ran from the machine and under a closed doorway in the courtyard wall.

'What does that thing do?' I shouted.

'I've no idea.'

As we drew further away from the noise Moishe turned to me.

'It's been there several months and is generally referred to as the college reactor.'

Moishe introduced me to Clarence Cohen, the head of my department. His office looked out over the courtyard we had just crossed. From my chair I could see its central pit and could still dimly hear rumbling.

After the formalities, Professor Cohen turned towards Moishe.

'Did you hear the news this morning? Terrible, terrible. A young couple on holiday in Yellowstone Park were sleeping in their vehicle, some sort of van, I think. They left the door open. A bear came in the night and ripped off the side of the young man's face. They made the mistake of keeping their food beside them. The bear must have smelt it.'

'No, Clarence, I didn't hear the story. I must have been in the shower.'

That morning I also met Steven Redman, a member of Moishe's department and his best friend.

'So, you've come to pursue your studies at the cultural capital of the world, the heart of art.' He let out a burst of laughter.

'Ignore him, he's in one of his moods,' said Moishe, hanging up our coats.

We sat drinking coffee in Moishe's office, all on swivel chairs, each of us occasionally swinging to one side a few inches in punctuation of the conversation.

'I hear you're going to probe into the development of the New York School.' Steven was grinning at me unnervingly. I didn't know how to take him. 'The demographer's simple opinion is that all those European émigrés who fled here with the rise of fascism finally shattered our artistic parochialism.' He paused. 'But Moishe feels it was all due to good old American chutzpah.'

'Chutzpah?'

'Ask the Jew to define it for you.'

'Nerve, chutzpah means nerve.' Moishe too was grinning. 'You see, Steve; what did I tell you about Australians?'

'But Moishe, can we generalise?'

I must have looked uncomfortable, because Moishe slapped me on the arm.

'We play; you'll get used to this.'

'And we'll try to show you a good time,' said Steven; 'when we have time. What are your interests? What can this city offer you?'

'He is ignorant of jazz.'

'No?' Steven shook his head solemnly. 'What about old movies? Moishe and I often go into the city on our free afternoons and take in a movie or two at the revival houses. Do you like old movies?'

ELEVEN
PERVERSION

'Today I finally got sick of men.'

'I find that hard to believe.'

'I had an appraisal, arranged over the phone. When I arrived at the house the door was opened by a man wearing nothing but an apron. When I turned to leave he tried to grab me.' Elizabeth was standing at the kitchen counter, and waved a carving knife in the air as she spoke. Moishe leant back in a chair, his feet on the kitchen table. I was washing some dishes. The overhead light-fitting rattled in time with the bass drum as Ruth practised upstairs.

'Have you ever noticed it's always men who are the perverts?'

'I don't know. Isn't life all about fucking? Try being a man and you'll meet the horny women, the depraved and perverted, the wonderful.' Moishe was rocking on his chair.

'Don't give me that shit. How many women sexually assault or rape men?'

'I wasn't talking about aggression, I was talking about perversion.'

TWELVE
ENCYCLOPÆDIA

'Can you tell me anything about Frick?'

'About what?'

'You know, the Frick Museum, the man who started it.'

'Yes. His daughter still runs the place, I know that much. I think her name is Faith or Grace, something Victorian anyway. Women aren't admitted into the reading room of the library unless they're wearing skirts. In the era of blue jeans Miss Frick still has her way.' Moishe seemed to find this extremely amusing. 'But apart from that I know nothing, nothing at all about her daddy.'

Moishe and I were sitting in the living-room. He had just played me what he called some 'essential jazz': Eric Dolphy playing flute and alto saxophone.

'How about we look Frick up in the encyclopædia?' He got up from his chair and went over to the bookshelves, which covered the whole wall adjoining the dining-room. Among the densely packed clutter of coloured spines the volumes of the encyclopædia stood out as an ordered stretch of white and brown.

'I love looking things up in the encyclopædia.' Moishe's enthusiasm had a self-mocking undertone. 'Here he is: ''Frick, Henry Clay, 1849 to 1919''. The perfect dates for an American self-made millionaire. Alright, I'll read you it: ''US industrialist, art collector and philanthropist, was born at West Overton, Pennsylvania, December 19, 1849. He organised the firm Frick and Company, 1871, acquired extensive coal deposits, built about twelve thousand coke ovens and supplied the Pittsburgh steel mills with the coke that city required for its steel and iron industry. During the Homestead, Pennsylvania, steel strike of 1892 Frick was shot and stabbed by Alexander Berkman, an anarchist, but survived. He was chairman of the board of Carnegie Brothers, 1889 to '92, and a director of a number of railroads and of US Steel Corporation. Frick died in New York City on December 2, 1919. He left a park to Pittsburgh with an endowment and established the H.C. Frick Educational foundation. He bequeathed his New York town house to that city with numerous paintings, bronzes and enamels. He also endowed many hospitals and educational and charitable institutions." ' Moishe looked up at me and then back at the book. 'How about this: "Friction is the resistance which is offered to the sliding of one solid body over another. From earliest times man has made ingenious attempts to diminish it . . ." What *would* we do without the encyclopædia!'

THIRTEEN
TELEVISION

I picture the Feinbaums' house from the street; it is sliced open in cross-section like a doll's house. This night there was only one light on in the whole building and that was in the kitchen. But there was no one in that room. The rest of the house was in darkness but for a flickering of faint grey light in the living-room. As my eyes adjust I am able to pick out the members of the family arranged in front of the television. They were gathered close together on a long built-in sofa, with rugs spread on their knees, their faces concentrated and weirdly lit by the everchanging colourless light.

For Moishe there were three basic rules for television watching. Already, early in my stay, I had heard two debates over colour television. For Moishe there was no such thing. Television was black and white. It was that simple. The children could make no progress with their desire for colour. Everyone else might have colour television, it might be more realistic, even inexpensive, the reception of the old black and white set might be shaky; but Moishe was unmoved. In fact he was threatening to buy a new black and white set. Another rule concerned lighting. Successful television viewing was done in the dark. There might be light in another room, preferably kitchen, but nothing nearer. The third rule required food. A happy evening of viewing involved regular snacks. For Moishe the television advertisement was invented for the preparation of food, and possibly for urination.

That evening the whole family was watching television. There had been considerable jockeying for seating. Both Herman and Ruth wanted to sit between their parents. Moishe proclaimed loudly how essential it was that his wife should cleave to him throughout the evening's entertainment, but eventually gave way to Herman, who adroitly insinuated his way between them. Ruth ended up sulking beside her father. Meanwhile I found myself sitting comfortably between Elizabeth and Hannah. Blankets and quilts were tugged into position over our laps and legs.

We were waiting for the evening movie. We had gathered early and were watching whatever was on, whatever channel the children had selected. We had abandoned ourselves to the evening, to the mood of time happily squandered on entertainment, recklessly. The movie to be was *Casablanca*. Moishe had preliminary comments.

'How many times have you seen this goddam movie?' he asked me, leaning forward and looking at me past Elizabeth.

'Three or four, I think.'

'Exactly. Have you read *War and Peace*?'

'Yes.' Already I knew Moishe well enough to realise he was leading me somewhere.

'In what circumstances?'

'Circumstances?'

'Yes. Where were you? What were you doing at the time?'

'I was in hospital having my appendix taken out.'

Moishe clapped his hands, letting out a little laugh of satisfaction.

'Nearly everyone I know has been ill when they've read *War and Peace*. I had a bad flu, Elizabeth's leg was in a cast, Steve had pneumonia and so on. Some graduate student should write a thesis on "The effect of pain on the interpretation of Leo Tolstoy's *War and Peace*".'

'What's all this got to do with *Casablanca*?' asked Hannah, impatiently.

'If *War and Peace* can't be read without pain then *Casablanca* can't be seen without familiarity. I've seen it probably a dozen times. How many times have you seen it, honey?'

'Oh, four or five.' Elizabeth smiled mysteriously.

'I've only seen it once.' Hannah was defiant.

'That doesn't matter, you've heard so much about it, you know the famous lines, you've heard "As Time Goes By" how many times? You know about Humphrey Bogart, you know about Ingrid Bergman.'

'Do you people have to talk so much? I haven't seen this movie.' Ruth said this while trying to pull the rug off Moishe's lap in punishment for his loquacity. Meanwhile the movie had begun, a little shakily. It was a well-worn print.

As the film picked up momentum I felt Elizabeth's thigh on my left and Hannah's on my right relax against mine. I glanced to my left along the line of profiles, of bodies snugly bundled up. I was conscious of being a part of this family's intimacy. Elizabeth's profile was beautiful in the eerie light, vulnerable in her concentration. Even Moishe seemed to have put aside his personality, his face looking somehow naked. Then I realised he had taken off his glasses and was cleaning them with a tissue. His hands moved deftly even though he watched the screen. He slipped his glasses back on and again was clothed. I looked around at Hannah, who looked at me at the same time. She seemed to frown and smile at once. She shifted away from me slightly.

As the advertising breaks became longer the subject of food arose. Herman and Ruth pleaded for hot chocolate with floating marshmallows. Moishe asked for a beer with paté and crackers. Hannah wanted coffee and some cookies. Herman and Ruth wanted cookies too. I listened to these orders being made into plain air, or so it seemed, until Elizabeth untangled herself from her quilt and assumed the role of provider.

I look down on my memory, from the street. The house, opened up to my gaze, was in darkness. I see Herman's unmade bed. The crumpled sheets formed a desert landscape strewn with comic books, and dimly lit by white street-light through the windows. In Ruth's room the bleached light glistened on her cymbals and across the skin of her side drum. Hannah's door was shut, the curtains drawn, the room absolutely dark. In the kitchen Elizabeth was stirring a saucepan of chocolate milk with a whisk; she leant against the stove, her wrist moving with consummate ease. In the living-room the family remained clustered together throughout the commercials, staring at the small source of light, as though trying to fit these unlikely subplots into the overall pattern of the movie itself.

FOURTEEN
HOMESTEAD: THE BATTLE

Before I arrived in New York I knew of the Frick Museum and was aware of several of the great paintings in the collection, particularly the Vermeers and the late Rembrandt self-portrait in which the painter depicted himself in exotic clothes, his left hand on a cane. This was a wonderful painting. As for Frick himself, somewhere I had heard or read briefly of the strike at Homestead. Andrew Carnegie, the Carnegie steel company's major shareholder, was away on holiday in Scotland and had left Frick in charge of the mills. During the strike, private guards were called in by Frick and some of the strikers were shot. This was my memory. With my background in a family preoccupied by politics and social justice the fact that I remembered Frick at all was probably due to a reaction of repugnance to his role in the Homestead strike. Politics was possibly the only factor capable of disturbing my family's closeness. The sacking of the Whitlam government in 1975 brought my parents near to estrangement, not because their views differed, but because they were both emotionally drained by the crisis. Their tempers flared for months. Subsequently my mother could not see Malcolm Fraser in the paper or hear his voice on the radio without becoming irritable. At the age of fifteen I 'marched for democracy', candle in hand, during the election campaign that followed the sacking.

A few days after Moishe read to me about Frick from the encyclopædia I borrowed several books from the college library. They included volume two of Phillip S. Foner's *History of the Labor Movement in the United States* and *Organized Labor in American History* by Philip Taft. Now that I was in America and had seen Frick's legacy on Seventieth Street, my memory of Homestead interested me. How accurate was it? And how relevant to my studies was the story of Frick's industrial and cultural activities? I took the books to bed with me in the basement. That night the house was quiet. The children were in their rooms. Moishe was listening to jazz in the living-room and the music faintly filtered down to me. Every now and then the furnace would click and then roar alight, rumble deeply for several minutes and just as suddenly cut out.

I have recently re-read the relevant chapters from most of the books I took to bed with me that night. All of them were written from the standpoint of the history of the labour movement. I could find nothing, beyond encyclopædia entries, on Frick himself. What follows is an attempt to reconstruct the various accounts into one.

Pittsburgh, Pennsylvania; Detroit, Michigan; Boston, Massachusetts; Denver, Colorado; Nashville, Tennesee; Salt Lake City, Utah; Savannah, Georgia; New York, New York. I say these names together and I am immediately transported to the heart of my memory of the United States. This is not because I remember these places. I have never been to most of them. It is because the pairing of these names seems intrinsically American. Nowhere else in the world could Paris be referred to as Paris, France. And this is not merely because there is a Paris, Texas. The events at Homestead, too, seem fundamentally American. Could Henry Clay Frick have lived in any other country?

In the centre of the city of Pittsburgh, Pennsylvania, is the junction of the Monongahela and Allegheny rivers, which thereafter become the Ohio. In 1871 the Homestead Bank and Life Insurance Company looked upstream from Pittsburgh along the Monongahela river some seven miles. The company bought a number of farms and divided them in the hope of developing a commuter suburb of Pittsburgh. The following year the new township of Homestead was connected with Pittsburgh by rail. In 1876 industry arrived in the form of a glass factory and this was followed in 1881 by a steel mill, built on the riverbank. It was this steel mill which was taken over in 1886 by the Carnegie Company.

Concurrent but certainly not coincidental with these events was the formation, in 1876, of the Amalgamated Association of Iron and Steel workers of America. Between 1876 and 1885 the Amalgamated authorised 93 strikes; of these twenty-eight were successful, four were compromised and sixty-one failed.

When the year 1892 opened the workers at the Homestead mill were paid under an agreement which was due to expire on the thirtieth of June. Wages rose and fell according to the market price of steel but were protected by a floor, of twenty-five dollars per ton, below which they could not slip.

On the fourth of April Andrew Carnegie wrote to his

Chairman Henry Frick from Scotland. The letter remained undisclosed until 1903.

As the vast majority of our employees are non-union, the firm has decided that the minority must give place to the majority. These works, therefore, will be necessarily non-union after the expiration of the present contract.

Frick met the union and handed the committee a pay scale with an average reduction of twenty-two per cent and a rescheduling of the contract expiry date from the thirtieth of June to the first of January. The company wanted to avoid its vulnerability to strikes in summer, the time of peak production. Frick gave the union until the twenty-fourth of June to accept and announced that 'these scales are in all respects the most liberal that can be afforded'.

Henry Clay Frick, wrote Philip Taft,

. . . was the personification of the ruthless business leader who would tolerate no opposition. His attitude towards labor was uncompromising. Once having decided to solve an issue by economic power, he crushed all who questioned his decision, with the aid if necessary of the coal and iron police, the Pinkertons and the state militia.

Frick began his career as a clerk in a dry goods store. He later became a bookkeeper in his grandfather's distillery. But his great success came in the coke industry, where he made his first million. It was a logical step into the steel industry, financed by Carnegie and the chairman of his company.

I think it was probably at about this point in my reading that Frick began to assume importance for me beyond any obvious excuse my studies might have provided. If I were attracted by the broad patterns of history then I was easily seduced by its more quirkish moments. As I lay in bed I distinctly remembered something else about Frick, an anecdote I'd heard some time before from a guest at my family dinner table. Early this century Frick had given a Fourth of July dinner to Teddy Roosevelt. There had been eight courses. Some of the details had stuck with me. The meal began with melon. This was followed by soup, I couldn't remember what sort. Next came salmon, followed by sweetbread and peas. I remembered the sweetbread and peas because the idea of eating them was unpleasant. The fifth course was *filet Châteaubriand*, the sixth roast duck, the seventh cheese and biscuits and finally some sort of dessert. The thought of this meal remained with me through the rest of my reading: the American President dining so thoroughly with Frick and select guests on the fourth of July, the anniversary of American independence.

A conference was held between the union and the management of the Homestead mill on the twenty-third of June. Disagreement over the floor price per ton was narrowed to one dollar. Frick's position hardened at twenty-three dollars; the union held out for twenty-four. Neither side was willing to compromise over the contract expiry date.

On the twenty-fifth of June the company announced that its terms would be implemented regardless of the views of the Amalgamated. In a press interview Frick declared he would no longer deal with the union. The issue, he said, was 'whether the Carnegie Company or the Amalgamated Association shall have absolute control of our plant and business at Homestead'. He had meanwhile contacted Robert Pinkerton, head of the famous detective agency, and asked for three hundred guards to be assembled at some point:

. . . on the Ohio river below Pittsburgh, where they can be transferred to boats and landed within the enclosures of our premises at Homestead. We think absolute secrecy essential in the movement of these men so that no demonstration can be made while they are en route.

Between the evening of the twenty-eighth and the morning of the twenty-ninth the steel mill was shut down by its management. A mass meeting of workers, both skilled and unskilled, was held, and despite their mutual antagonism all 3,800 men decided to strike. An advisory committee was elected with Hugh O'Donnell as chairman. Constant shifts were organised to guard the riverbank. A steam launch and a number of skiffs patrolled the river. Strangers in town were questioned and those with inadequate explanations were forced to leave. Reporters were issued with identification and were expelled for writing negative reports. Headquarters were set up and telegraph communications established to allow warning of strike-breakers. Even the saloon keepers were visited and asked to prevent excessive drinking.

On the fourth of July the local sheriff was called in by the company. He approached the town but was turned away after refusing to deputise a number of strikers to keep order.

During the night of the fifth of July the three hundred Pinkertons boarded two barges five miles below Pittsburgh. While being towed upstream by a tug, improbably called the *Little Bill*, they changed into their blue uniforms and were armed with Winchester rifles.

Despite the attempt at secrecy a warning cable arrived at Homestead. A steam whistle, sounded in alarm, brought the strikers and townspeople down to the riverbank. Following the steam launch and skiffs downstream they reached the mill as the barges drew near. The mill had been fortified and the crowd broke down a fence before they rushed through the mill yard to the landing.

As the barges drew into the bank they were warned back by the shouting strikers. The captain in charge of the Pinkertons declared that he was taking over the works and the crowd must leave. This was answered with shouts of defiance. A gangplank was lowered and several Pinkertons began to come ashore. A striker leapt forward to block them. A first shot was fired, quickly followed by a second. The Pinkertons then fired a volley into the crowd. For some minutes gunfire continued from both sides while the guards retreated into their barges and the strikers behind the stacks of steel on the landing.

Two hours later there was another effort to land and the shooting began again. Oil-soaked boxes and barrels were set alight and rolled down a siding into the river, oil was poured onto the water, and even dynamite was thrown at the barges, all in an unsuccessful attempt to destroy them. The *Little Bill* tried to rescue the barges but was shot at and retreated.

After several hours, the Pinkertons raised a white flag. It was ignored until Hugh O'Donnell, the workers' chairman intervened to arrange surrender terms. Safe passage was assured, but in fact the guards were beaten by the angry crowd on the way to the town's skating rink where they were kept. The barges were stripped of everything valuable, covered with oil and burnt. The battle had lasted from 4.00am until 5.00pm. Approximately nine workers and three Pinkertons were killed.

These events made nationwide headlines. One editorial writer, in terms typical of the general reaction, described the strikers as 'savage beasts who deserve no pity'. By contrast the unions gave support. A union organiser in New Orleans wrote that the strikers 'have the sympathy of all laboring men down here and the only fault I have heard expressed is that they left a living Pinkerton'. Union resolutions referred to 'the hired thugs of many times millionaire Carnegie' and called upon Congress 'for the suppression of this vast army of the capitalist class'.

FIFTEEN
WARBURGS 2

Moishe and I were sitting in the Volkswagen in the Warburgs carpark. We had driven there to do the shopping but we were still in the car, talking. Lake Warburgs was dry. A cold wind was blowing and we watched the people who came and went from the supermarket, their skirts, hair and coats given independent life by the air-currents.

'Look at that,' said Moishe pointing out a young woman whose skirt was trying to escape between her legs. 'Now there's a true case of clothing enhancing the human figure. Look at the way the cloth hugs her legs, gives them suggestive volume. The naked legs themselves could only be less real.' The woman had disappeared through the automatic doors. Several people stood outside the doors, waiting for taxis. They hugged their coats to their bodies among a crowd of shopping carts.

'It has been suggested to me that I have a roving eye. Not that Elizabeth has ever accused me, she's not the type. My wife is totally devoid of jealousy, which is something that has disappointed me on a number of occasions. At times my ego would like to be flattered by a little possessiveness. Take Steve's wife, Natalie; she is capable of being affronted if he expresses admiration for a movie actress under the age of seventy-five.'

A man passed us nearby. I recognised him. He was the man I had seen on the night of my arrival, passing me outside the drugstore. He still wore the torn, checked lumber-jacket. On his feet he had green plastic bags, folded until they were many layers thick and tied around the ankles with strips of cloth. He entered Warburgs.

'I love my wife.' Moishe turned his head and looked at me as he said this. I simply had no idea what to say, which in conversation with Moishe was rarely a disadvantage. But I was aware now of a peculiar light in his eyes which suggested he was testing me in some way. I tried to imagine his personal variety of love and then thought of various friends, from my recently completed days as an undergraduate student, who went through periods of obsessively romantic or vigorously sexual activity. It had seemed to me that their studies, their families, their friends became mere distractions then. Love often made them vague, irritable, inarticulate, preoccupied, or erratically euphoric. All this had largely sidestepped me and I admit my tolerance for passion was limited. And here I was being obliquely challenged by this announcement, from a man who had been married almost as long as I had been alive, that he loved his wife.

'Doesn't it seem weird to you that I should love my wife?'

'No, not at all.'

'Look at those two.' Moishe was again distracted by arriving shoppers, two young women this time. 'Winter is a time of such disguises. Somewhere behind those coats, sweaters and winter underwear lie variations on the inevitable undulations of the female body. Would you believe it now? You have to exercise considerable imagination. It is depressing how much imagination is required. We must try to remember that other shopper's legs where even winter clothing played another role. Have you ever considered breasts? I mean closely considered breasts and clothing? There are stages, a series of points on a flexible scale, that I call the zone of enhanced possibilities, intimated pleasures. This is where cloth reveals more than it hides.'

I smiled and looked at the women, trying to see them as Moishe did. This frank voyeurism was new to me. People, and that essentially meant my family and a few friends, were familiar beings largely separate from the visual analysis which was a major part of my studies. Of course, I had looked at women before but in nothing like this conscious way.

'We must come and sit here together in the summer and make some clear comparisons, OK?'

'I look forward to it. Is this an educational project?'

'Maybe. It's more an exercise in sensual indulgence. After all, what do you learn watching people? If you're an optimist you find all sorts of human warmth. If you're a misanthrope you see debasement and ugliness. If you're a normal guy, like me, you notice the pretty girls.'

'I thought perhaps that you were some sort of latter day physiognomist.'

'Me? Well maybe I am. But I draw no conclusions about character. I enjoy comparing the attributes of all these people. Come on, let's go shopping.'

It was Friday afternoon and Warburgs was packed with shoppers stocking up for the weekend or before the Sabbath prohibition on work after sundown on Friday. Once, out walking, I had been stopped by a small, nervous man outside an Orthodox Jewish temple. He had wanted me to turn on the air-conditioner. It was Saturday morning and no one in the temple could touch the switch.

So, Warburgs was packed. Near the cash registers the aisles were jammed with shopping carts. Moishe pushed ahead and I followed with a cart. We turned a corner just in time to see someone collide with a tall stack of imported canned tomatoes. The stack toppled, and most of it was neatly collected by a passing cart. Crushed eggs began to drip through the bottom of the cage.

'You fuckin' jerk, can't you look where you're goin'!'

'Don't you fuckin' jerk me, you fuckin' jerk.'

The two men, both short and thickset, both in their sixties or seventies, both wearing overcoats and hats, stood at their carts glaring at each other. A pair of hands with whitened knuckles gripped the push-bar of each cart.

As we left them behind, receding into the canyon perspective of the aisle, Moishe chuckled and turned to me.

'A visit to Warburgs is like a military campaign. Every manoeuvre is subject to sabotage, ambush, breakdown in communications, bottle necks, and cut supply lines. Primarily cut supply lines.' Moishe had stopped for flour and found the whole shelf was empty. 'Flour, is it or isn't it a staple? How will I explain this to Elizabeth, the queen of baked goods, the empress of bread, the doyenne of the homemade cookie?'

'You're saved.' I had seen a lone packet of flour misplaced with the white sugar and reached for it.

'You're good, by God. The boy is good. Thank you. While you're bringing me such luck would you go to the frozen food section? You know the frozen food section? See if your luck can find me some shrimp amongst the chaos of the freezers. I can never find it.'

I found the shrimp, almost immediately, but also a rotten banana, which had somehow made its way from the fruit and vegetable department, at the other end of the supermarket, and was now lying, slimy and black, on top of the pile of boxes of frozen shrimp.

I walked back, looking for Moishe, passing the meat chillers which stretched along the whole back wall. The meat, wrapped in plastic and resting in styrofoam trays, glistened moistly, its red generously marbled with white fat. Some of the reds were tinged grey. Housewives prodded at the packets, searching for expiry date and weight labels. Piles of plucked, plastic-wrapped chickens, corn fed and yellow skinned, had been raked over continuously and lay awkwardly, legs in the air, severed necks livid. A man was poking the chickens with a pencil. He noticed me watching him.

'I always carry a pencil. You see,' he said, prodding at a fat bird, 'you pop the plastic and then you smell if they're fresh or not.'

I found Moishe among the fruit and vegetables. He looked up as I approached.

'They call these beans. Do you call these beans?' He held up a limp and yellowed bean for my disapproval. 'I call these has-beans. Come on, I've got all we want, if not all we need.'

We pushed our way to the jam at the cash registers. People with piles of shopping queued at the express lines. Others forced their way into line either with guile or bravado. There was no one to bag the groceries at Warburgs, yet customers stood hands on hips or fumbling with their handbags. They waited for their groceries to be packed, into brown paper bags, by the person who worked the cash register.

'Look at this pageant of human types.' Moishe was talking so loudly that many of the people he was looking at must clearly have heard him. 'Nearly all these people are either Jewish or Irish. Island City has only three, roughly equal size, racial groups: Jewish, Irish and black. But the blacks live at the north-east end of the island. No one will sell or rent to them here, so the blacks you see are either out shopping or they work as somebody's cleaner. So we're left with the Jews and the Irish. They basically hate each other. No, it's true. The Jews think the Irish are drunken, fornicating, lazy, Christian bastards and the Irish think the Jews money grabbing, cheap, Zionist pigs. We all live side by side in self-indulgent intolerance. Look at that man in the far line, the one wearing the baseball cap. The big gut, the free and easy stance, the lumber-jacket; he's all Irish American. You'll see others like him every time you come here. And that woman in the fur coat. See, she's wearing a hair net. She looks small and ill but don't be misled. She's anyone's equal in an argument. She's Jewish American, a living cliché.'

A man in the next line was watching Moishe belligerently. Moishe noticed him.

'Sorry; you don't enjoy my outrageous generalisations?'

'Fuck you, mac.' He gave our cart a shove and it ran into my ankle.

On our way home, driving back along Bayside Drive, Moishe suddenly returned the conversation to Elizabeth.

'Do you think my wife is a plain woman?'

'You're joking.'

'You find her attractive? I think she is plain. I can tell you this because I've told her.'

I sat in silence, totally inadequate to this situation.

'Perhaps I can explain myself. I love Elizabeth, I am attracted by her, I think she is plain.' Moishe chuckled. 'Some explanation, huh?'

'Perhaps I understand you.'

Moishe laughed. 'Elizabeth is the greatest.' As he said this we turned into the Feinbaums' street.

SIXTEEN
HOMESTEAD: THE DEFEAT

Where in the history of the radical minded labour organizations of Europe is it possible to find chapters comparable to Homestead . . .?

Jack Barbash

Steel Workers, fighting a losing battle against the growing steel trust, drove away the Pinkerton thugs in armed struggle and seized the local steel mills, rifles in hand.

William Foster

Following the battle at Homestead the town was firmly in control of the union. The strikers were confident. Governor Robert E. Pattison had not sent in the State Militia to break the strike. The press generally reported that the situation at Homestead was peaceful. The American Federation of Labor organised picketing of the labour recruitment agencies in New York and other major cities. Furthermore, workers at other Carnegie plants went out on strike. A worker from the union Mills plant explained the situation:

> It is not our battle we are fighting but for organised labor. They signed our scale, but we knew we would be the next victim . . . Homestead is the stronghold and should Mr. Frick win the strike there nothing will be left for us but to fall in line.

Meanwhile the company issued statements to the press, asserting that the violence had decided one matter forever:

> . . . that the Homestead mill hereafter will be run non-union, and the Carnegie Company will never again recognise the Amalgamated Association nor any other labor organization.

The local sheriff continued to make calls for state troops, claiming that 'Only a large military force will enable me to control matters.' On the tenth of July, four days after the battle, Governor Pattison ordered Major General George R. Snowden to assemble the National Guard of Pennsylvania, numbering eight thousand, and move to Homestead. It later became clear that Pattison's decision was due to the successful management of the borough by the union and the fear that this might set a precedent in other industrial cities. Major General Snowden expressed the attitude: 'Philadelphians can hardly appreciate the actual communism of these people. They believe the works are theirs as much as Carnegie's.' He described the strike as 'revolution, treason and anarchy'.

The troops cleared the Homestead mill of the strikers and

remained in the town until the thirteenth of October. At first the strikers accepted the intervention of the troops as a neutral assertion of order. When Snowden's comments became widely publicised and the militia began to escort strike breaking labour into the mill, attitudes rapidly changed. The company had more than seventy employment agencies searching the whole country for skilled labour. Special bonuses and railway tickets were offered as inducements.

The furnaces were relit on the fifteenth of July. The company knew it could not produce steel of any quality with limited scab labour. Training a new workforce would be slow and costly. In fact, what the company wanted was to re-hire the strikers on its own terms. On the sixteenth of July an announcement was made that individual applications would be received until the twenty-first, after which all new men would be employed. In a further angle of attack, seven of the strike leaders were charged with murder on the eighteenth of July. They spent the night in jail and were released on ten thousand dollars bail.

The union retaliated with murder charges against officials of the Carnegie Company and the Pinkerton Agency. Ten thousand dollars bail was allowed without the defendants having to spend the night in jail.

Late in July Hugh O'Donnell, without the knowledge of the union membership, approached Whitelaw Reid, the publisher of the New York Tribune and a leading conservative. He asked Reid to intervene with the company. The strikers, he said, were not committed upon any question of scale, wages or hours, if the company would return to negotiation. After the strike ended Andrew Carnegie maintained he had wanted O'Donnell's offer considered but he actually cabled 'nothing can be done'. Communicating from his lodge in Scotland he made little comment but to say that he had 'implicit confidence in those who are managing the mills'. He later denied approval of the role of the Pinkertons: 'to my best knowledge and belief I never heard of such a thing. And of course

I did not know they were employed at Homestead at the time.'

The strike continued to hold surprisingly firmly. Weekly rallies were held in the skating rink to reinforce the workers' solidarity. On the thirtieth of August the company acted decisively. The members of the Amalgamated Advisory Committee were charged with conspiracy and riot. In total 167 workers were indicted. A bond, impossible to raise, of over half a million dollars was required for bail. The charges were made under a law dating to 1860 despite a Pennslyvania statute passed in 1891 making it lawful for workmen to strike without prosecution 'for conspiracy at common law or under criminal laws of the commonwealth'.

The strikers reacted by also charging the management of the company with riot and conspiracy. Frick and his associates had no difficulty obtaining bail from the Pittsburgh bankers, Andrew and Richard Mellon.

The company, meanwhile, with considerable shrewdness, based its charges not on the events of the sixth of July but on the 'usurpation of civil authority' at Homestead between that date and the arrival of the National Guard. Chief Justice Paxton of the State Supreme Court intervened in the cases due to their 'supreme importance'. He blamed the problem on:

> . . . the addition of large numbers of foreigners to our labouring population. Many of them are densely ignorant, as well as brutal in their dispositions. They have false ideas of the kind of liberty we enjoy in this country. It is needed that all such persons should be taught this lesson that our liberty is the liberty of law not the liberty of license.

He concluded:

> We have reached a point where there are but two roads left for us to pursue; the one leads to order and good government, the other leads to anarchy.

The union leadership was forced to spend much of its time and energy on legal defence and manoeuvring. The limited strike fund was rapidly drained by bail and legal expenses. Many of the organisers not arrested went into hiding. Sixteen hundred workers were on the relief rolls at a cost of ten thousand dollars a week. Contributions began to dwindle and the strikers and their families to suffer from shortages of food and clothing. Press reports began to appear of strikers leaving Homestead for work elsewhere and of some applying for and receiving employment in the mill itself.

By mid-October the mood of the strikers was shifting. There was a sense that their cause was lost. Faith in the American Federation of Labor and in the Amalgamated Advisory Committee and its willingness to act faltered. Indeed, the Committee had backed off from applying to the Federation for a boycott of material manufactured by the Carnegie Company. The union officials, acting too late, decided to organise an appeal to the American public for contributions on the thirteenth of December 1892, to be known as 'Homestead Day'. Scattered contributions began to come in as early as the sixteenth of November.

On the eighteenth of November mechanics and day labourers at Homestead met and asked to be released from the strike. In response the unionists met and although voting to stay out themselves notified their unskilled colleagues to do as they liked. The mechanics and day labourers as a gesture voted not to take tonnage jobs but decided unanimously to return to work. Immediately the rush back to the mill was on. Charles M. Schwab, Frick's newly appointed company superintendant, had the men lined up for consideration. He chose a number and told the others their jobs were filled.

The Amalgamated met again on the twentieth of November, its membership depleted. Many men had left Homestead; O'Donnell and others were in jail. When the question was put to declare the strike off and the mill open it was carried by a vote of 101 to 91.

Next morning there was a second rush for jobs. Again the men were made to line up before Charles Schwab. Their names were checked off in a book containing a list of the most active strikers. Some workers were re-employed for two dollars a twelve-hour day when before the strike the rate had been four dollars for eight hours. Many other men were turned away.

In this way the four and a half month struggle ended. The accused workers, including Hugh O'Donnell, were acquitted except for two cooks who were convicted for poisoning non-union men at the mills. The charges against Frick, fifteen company officials and the two heads of the Pinkerton Agency were dismissed.

From 1892 not a single union man was employed at a Carnegie mill for the next forty-five years. Membership of the union dropped from 20,975 in 1892 to 10,000 in 1894, and to 6,295 in 1909. The twelve-hour shift rapidly replaced its eight-hour predecessor, at first in the Carnegie plants and then in the rest of the industry. Sunday labour, rare before the strike, became usual.

Frick, writing to Carnegie after his victory, commented that 'The firmness with which these strikers held on is surprising.'

SEVENTEEN
REMBRANDT

The dining-room table was round. The wood was dark, elegant and appeared to have been finished with considerable craftsmanship.

'You really built this thing yourself?'

'Yes Moishe.' Steven's tone suggested that the conversation was being replayed.

'You're amazing, you know that don't you. A creator in this paradise of debauched consumerism.'

Steven looked at me across the table.

'This performance is for your benefit.'

'Don't be so ungenerous. This is admiration from a man who can't tell a hammer from a wrench.' Moishe ran his hand along the edge of the table with mock tenderness.

'And is proud of it.' Steven still faced me, although both men's attention was directed by inference to Elizabeth and to Natalie, Steven's wife, for whom they appeared to be performing. 'Your host belongs to a rapidly growing class of perfectly able human beings who have decided to have nothing to do with physical activity beyond sport and sex. These people fancy their incapability somehow makes them cute.'

'Today you have to specialise. I decided to concentrate on sex.'

'Moishe, are we supposed to be amused?'

'Natalie, can I really help it if women long to use my body as their plaything?'

Steven Redman and Natalie Bush lived only three streets away from the Feinbaums, but on the beach block overlooking the flat expanse of the Atlantic. Their house was small, built in the 1920s as a summer bungalow for a middle-class family from Brooklyn. It had become run down, like many houses in the area, as Island City's status as a seaside resort slipped after the war. Steven and Natalie had moved here in the mid-seventies. They were part of a wave of middle-class reinvestment in the island. Or so Moishe told me as he, Elizabeth and I walked over to have dinner with Steven and Natalie one evening late in the winter. I remember the air was without its previous vicious bite and the twilight was lingering faintly.

'These young people brought their ideal of a Manhattan apartment out here to rebuild and redecorate houses they could afford. Some of them are still here, enclaves of fashion amongst the drab suburbanism of our regular population. Steve and Natalie were pretty unique in that they did most of the work on their place themselves. It's impressive, you'll see.'

The five of us were seated at the table. Steven had cooked pasta, fettucine marinara. There was garlic bread and there was salad. In the serving bowls and on our plates the pasta steamed, the bread exuded fragrance and the salad glistened.

Elizabeth and Natalie were discussing a recently released film. Moishe was scornful.

'You people who have to see the latest movie are taking entertainment all wrong.'

'We all know about your retrogressive opinions,' said Natalie.

'I call it perspective. A movie should be a little dated, slightly tacky and unbelievable. All these people addicted to our entertainment industry with its special effects are like Romans at the circus crying out for fresh blood.'

'What about the catharsis of vicarious violence?'

'What about it?'

'What about real-life circuses?' interjected Steven. 'I've got a story for you, about the Bar Mitzvah Walter Rosenberg from Computing gave his little Eric a couple of weeks ago. It was a Safari Bar Mitzvah, in Park Slope, everyone wore jungle outfits. There were wild animals in the apartment, real animals but in cages. Eric gave demonstrations of his skill with a bull-whip in the bathroom.' Steven turned to me. 'You know what a Bar Mitzvah is?'

'The Jewish coming of age?'

'Sure. Eric came of age when he cracked the bathroom mirror, six feet by four feet. The party cost twenty-five thousand dollars all up. That's what Walter claims, anyway.'

'That's insane.' Natalie leant back in her chair, shaking her head. In what I was discovering to be an American habit, the house was overheated, and Natalie was wearing a tee-shirt. I thought of Moishe's theory of the enhancement of flesh through clothing. The tee-shirt had 'Island City College' printed on the front. The *I* and *D* of Island crossed her breasts. Indeed, her left nipple was neatly enclosed within the *D* and visible beneath the cloth. Perhaps I could understand Moishe, after all. Would Natalie's breasts have been less alluring when totally revealed?

'Talking of insanity,' said Elizabeth. 'I had a crazy case today.'

'Oh, here we go with one of your realty sex loons,' said Moishe. ' "House-owning Perverts of America".'

'I had an appraisal. His name was Dumplenicker. I mean Dumplenicker! Why aren't the weird ones Kelly or Cohen? Mr Dumplenicker answered the door fully clothed and I thought that maybe I was set for an easy time. Anyway, we started measuring the rooms; I was holding one end of my tape and Mr Dumplenicker the other. I noticed a needlepoint frame on a chair in the living-room, and women's underwear on a drying rack in the dining-room. In the kitchen there was a fancy spice cabinet full of jars neatly labelled in calligraphy.

I asked if his wife was the cook. I'd seen what I thought was some connection of style between the needlepoint, the lacy panties and the spice collection. He told me she *was* his wife, and looked at me so mournfully I felt embarrassed, as though *I* was intruding. I imagined Mrs Dumplenicker might have died earlier in the week, maybe after doing her washing. He then told me that his wife, her name was Roxanne, had left him two years ago.

'After that I was silent as we moved from room to room. In the bathroom there were cosmetics, a shower cap and robe. And then, in the bedroom, the closet doors were open, revealing the rack crammed full of dresses. Mr Dumplenicker told me they were all his wife's. He took out a long dress, black with leather trim. He held it to his chest and began to waltz around the bed, talking to me over his shoulder. He told me how he and Roxanne had adored dancing, at the ballroom, at home, everywhere. I'd backed up against the closet as he swept past me. He turned and glided up to me and asked: "Shall we dance?" '

Elizabeth took a sip of wine.

'Well, did you?' asked Natalie.

'Did I what?'

'Did you dance?'

'Or anything else?' added Moishe.

'Very funny, honey. I left the house real fast.'

'It amazes me you ever get to finish an appraisal,' said Moishe.

After dinner everyone was crowded into the kitchen, talking loudly. I wandered out into the living-room. Natalie, who was a commercial designer, had hand-painted the walls. They were soft grey with a repeated pattern of small, pastel pink and green spermatazoa-like squiggles. The room was sparsely furnished: a stereo, two sofas and some pot plants.

'How's your research going?' Steven had followed me from the kitchen.

'I'm not really sure.'

'How's that?'

'I attend my compulsory classes but otherwise I've been foraging in the rather distant past.' We both sat down on one of the sofas. 'I started reading about the 1892 strike at Homestead.'

'Homestead, Pennsylvania?'

'Yes, the steel strike.'

'What got you started on that?' He might have been mildly baiting me.

'Elizabeth took me to the Frick.'

'And one thing led to another.'

To my annoyance I felt myself blushing. Steven laughed.

'Do you know that Frick, when asked who he'd change places with in history, unhesitatingly chose Rembrandt?'

'How do you know that?' I asked, surprised by his knowledge but also intrigued by Frick's choice. Might there be more to Frick than I was allowing?

'There's a biography. Published by the museum, I think, if you're *that* seriously interested.'

'Are you sure it was Rembrandt that Frick chose?'

'I have the sort of brain that clearly retains such trivia. But what's so fascinating about Frick? Really, wasn't he just another nineteenth century industrialist who screwed his workers, collected art and donated it to the public to gain a sort of immortality?' He said this less as though discounting the possibility of Frick being unusual than challenging me to make Frick live for him as an individual. For the first time I felt a real sense of connection with Steven.

'Well that's the question. Do you know much about Homestead?'

'Frick was more ruthless than the average industrialist, is that what you mean?'

'Well, yes. I wonder about his business methods, and then

if his cultural aspirations were an attempt to legitimise his place in society.'

'That doesn't sound too outrageous.'

'Then I speculate about a wider social pattern; whether Frick's ambitions are typical of the powerbrokers in an emergent nation. Does this – and this is where my University work is supposed to come in – does this foreshadow the period of American cultural and political strength? In the late forties Modern Art was denounced in Washington as communistic and destructive to American traditions. But by the fifties the government was promoting Abstract Expressionism overseas as an arm of foreign policy. It was pushed in Europe perhaps as hard as Frick and his contemporaries had pulled European art across the Atlantic in the opening years of the century. And this embracing of radical art was going on at the height of the cold war and the persecution of political radicals at home.'

'Ah, I didn't know you had political obsessions as well.'

'And you?'

'Political obsessions?' Steve looked at me and smiled. 'Maybe we can talk about that another time. For now let's go have some coffee.'

EIGHTEEN
ATTEMPTED ASSASSINATION

We got home after midnight. The children had stayed up in front of the television, and the horror movie they'd watched had terrified Herman. He refused to go upstairs to bed for fear of what lurked unknown in the darkness. Everyone reassured him there was nothing there. Hannah went upstairs, with some reluctance it seemed to me, and turned on all the lights. Herman said nothing but shook his head. Finally Elizabeth picked him up and carried him to bed. Moishe put some jazz on the record player.

'That's a saxophone, isn't it?' I asked, bemused by the rich, flatulent honking of the solo instrument.

'Tenor sax, Sonny Rollins. It's a horn with a fabulous range and Rollins makes use of every note.'

I stood in the doorway listening for a minute and watching Moishe. He lounged in his chair, a glass of wine on the arm, his head lying back. Listening to music was the nearest I saw Moishe to abandonment.

Down in my room I could hear the saxophone as I undressed. I wanted to get into bed and re-read what information I had on the attempt on Frick's life. My conversation with Steven had stirred afresh my interest in the incident. Was it possible that I had missed in the various accounts of the attack some clue to Frick's character?

As I got into bed I heard the kitchen door open, followed by footsteps on the stairs. My room had no door and I saw

Elizabeth pass carrying the clothes basket. The laundry was also in the basement.

'Will it keep you awake if I put on a wash?' Her voice came from the next room.

'Not at all. I'll be reading for ages.'

'Are you decent?'

'As a human being?'

'We won't go into that. Are you clothed?'

'Yes.'

'Then may I come in and talk for a minute?' Various noises accompanied her voice, culminating in the banging of the washing machine lid and the sound of running water.

'Of course.'

Elizabeth came in and then stopped in the centre of the room, as though unsure of what she should do now that she was there.

'Please, sit down.'

'No, I'm fine thanks.'

Watching Elizabeth standing in the middle of the room reminded me of another image frozen in movement, another moment permanently separated from time. Whenever I recall it, the quality of the instant remains startling. I was bushwalking in quite thick eucalypt forest. I used to walk alone occasionally in my late teens. I had been following a ridge for some time, admiring a scattering of shattered and cracked grey boulders. I turned and dropped into a hollow. The trees were large here, some with trunks over a metre in diameter. There were clusters of bracken and maidenhair. And then, in front of me, standing back on its hind legs, was a swamp wallaby. We had not seen or heard each other until only several metres apart. We were transfixed by each other. The wallaby was absolutely motionless except for its forearms and paws moving rapidly, anxiously, in front of its chest. Then it bounded and was gone.

'Are you comfortable down here?'

'Completely.'

Was Moishe right? Was Elizabeth plain? What was plainness? She stood, her body isolated in space, in limbo between her last movement and her next.

'Did you get Herman to bed?'

'Yes he's OK. The others are asleep. Moishe is asleep in his chair . . . How's your reading on Frick?'

'It appears he really was the perfect corporate villain.'

'You suspected as much, didn't you.'

'Yes, but he doesn't seem to fit my expectations neatly enough.'

'In what way?'

'For a start, he wished he was Rembrandt.'

'Well I imagine Rembrandt had a pretty high profile then too. Wouldn't it be more surprising if he'd wanted to be a drag queen from a lower West Side bar?'

'I hadn't thought of it like that.'

Then Elizabeth moved.

'I'd better get Moishe to bed. Goodnight.'

'Goodnight.'

She stopped and turned in the doorway.

'You look cute in your pyjamas.'

I laughed. It reminded me that I intended to look up *cute* in the dictionary.

On the twenty-third of July, during the Homestead strike, at the height of the legal manoeuvring between the company and the union, Alexander Berkman, a young anarchist from New York, attacked Frick in his office.

Berkman, accompanied by two local anarchists, had inspected the company office in Pittsburg. The next day he entered the office alone and shot Frick twice. Frick caught hold of Berkman and, although wounded by both shots and then by stabs from his assailant's knife, wrestled with him until help came. Berkman surrendered himself, was tried and sentenced to twenty-five years jail, of which he served fourteen.

Frick's courage and rapid recovery won him considerable sympathy. Although the Advisory Committee of the union disassociated itself from the attack, the press connected Berkman with the strikers. The local police conducted an investigation. The police chief reported:

I am now satisfied that there was an organised movement against Frick, and Berkman was only a tool of a number of conspirators. . . There were more anarchists here than people supposed and they were getting ready to carry out some gigantic schemes.

A soldier, W.L. Iams, from the National Guard stationed at Homestead, called for 'three cheers for the man who shot Frick'. He was strung up by his thumbs until he apologised. He continued to refuse, was cut down and court martialled.

NINETEEN
BATHROOM

It was a weekday, early in the afternoon. I had just returned to the house from college. No one was home so I used the side door key I had been given for such occasions. The house had a quality of sudden departure, as though abandoned in emergency. A bowl on the kitchen table had some milk and a few soggy flakes of cereal left in it. The *New York Times* was spread out and there were bagel crumbs dotting its surface. Someone's sandwich and lunch juice had been left on the counter. Herman, I suspected, had had to beg from his friends again.

On the way down to my room I decided I would take this opportunity of free movement to quietly trim my beard at the large mirror in the upstairs bathroom. I collected my scissors and climbed the stairs.

Most middle-class families seem to have unwritten lists of things that will be done when time and money allow. The upstairs bathroom was on such a list for the Feinbaums. Its tiles, inherited from the previous owners, were pink and purple. In the afternoon, when the light was strongest through the window, the colours glowed with sickly intensity.

The room was basically clean but showed evidence that a family had hurriedly prepared for school and work. A wet tissue lay on the floor beside the wastepaper basket. The brown cardboard of a bare lavatory-paper roll remained in its dispenser. There was a small gob of toothpaste in the handbasin. And in the lavatory there was a fresh yellowish stain on the porcelin where a turd had slipped into the water.

I examined myself in the mirror, which was over the handbasin, and began clipping my beard. Because my face was clearly asymmetrical I had a decision to make. Would I make the cut lopsided in keeping with the jaw's underlying structure or follow some arbitrary sense of ordered form and make it perfectly symmetrical? I decided to cut quite close to my face, making a certain irregularity inevitable. Hair began to collect in the pink basin.

A door slammed downstairs. The noise startled me. I could hear Moishe's voice and, less distinctly, Elizabeth's. For some reason I felt uncomfortable, almost guilty, as though I were about to be discovered performing an illicit act. They were on the stairs now, their voices were clear.

'We could get a cleaning lady.'

'Look Moishe, I can continue to work and keep the house

reasonably clean or I can stop work and keep it like an operating theatre.'

They paused on the landing, outside the bathroom door.

'What time is it?' asked Moishe.

'One-fifteen.'

'We have time, before the kids get home, for a fuck.'

There were a few seconds silence.

'How about the shower?'

I stared at myself in the mirror and asked myself, for an instant, why this was happening. Then I started undressing, extremely rapidly and silently. I slipped into the shower, pulled the screen carefully shut and turned on the water. At first it was unbearably cold but I could no longer hear any noise from the other side of the door.

TWENTY
BIOGRAPHY

The Frick biography was not in the College library catalogue. I telephoned the Frick Collection and was told that the book was in stock.

I got off the subway at Fifty-ninth Street, on the East Side. This station was one of the most subterranean in the whole New York subway system and I felt vaguely claustrophobic as

I shuffled slowly with the morning rush-hour crowd towards the escalator.

Up on Lexington Avenue the sidewalk was crowded but there was room enough for me to weave a path at my own pace. I turned west, crossed Park Avenue and reached Madison. These famous names were now concrete determinants in my expanding exploration of the city. And they had a physical reality independent of reputation.

Park Avenue, for instance, was a broad corridor. I braced myself against an inevitable wind as I waited for traffic lights to change. Two men with a woman between them, all dressed professionally, stood ahead of me. They were talking with what I imagined to be bright office camaraderie. One of the men had extremely long legs, the woman had fat calves. I examined the backs of their heads. As the lights changed and we stepped off into the street I realised how much Moishe was affecting the way I looked at people.

Park Avenue was less an avenue of people than an avenue of atmosphere. Looking south, say from Sixty-fifth Street, the avenue dropped away slightly in a long panorama of lines, of facades, converging on the Pan Am Building in the distance. This view was always redefined by haze; sometimes the haze was the delicate white of morning, sometimes the crisp blue of a cold afternoon or the dull bruising of a summer dusk. At night the red tail-lights of the traffic charted the diminishing perspective of the avenue on one side, and on the other the glare of appraoching headlights defined its immediate scale.

On Madison I stopped at a book shop. The Frick Museum had yet to open, so I lingered looking at books in the art section. There was nothing on Frick nor, for that matter, anything of interest on the New York School. I began to pull out volumes at random. I flipped through a book titled *Art Students' Anatomy*. Something caught my attention. I leafed through the pages again, more slowly. One page showed nine little black and white photographs of a naked female figure in movement. In all nine photographs the woman's leading leg was the one nearest the viewer, thus obscuring her pubic area. I turned further pages. I could imagine Moishe looking with me, joining in this game. There were photographs of naked male and female archers, bows drawn back; and another of a male crouched for the start of a sprinting race, his hanging testicles obviously removed in an ineffective touch-up. I turned back to the front cover; here was a colour photograph of a male torso sensually lit from the side. Wasn't this misleading advertising? I looked for the original publication date on the first couple of pages. Copyright 1935, I found, and opposite this the dedication: 'To My Mother'. I smiled and leafed through the book again. On one page I read:

> The Mammary Gland or breast is rudimentary in the male. In the female the gland remains undeveloped from the first year (infancy) up to the fourteenth year (puberty), when it increases in size, for a time, due to greater blood supply and accumulation of fat.
>
> The gland measures about one half inch in diameter at puberty and is increased to over four inches in the adult. The thickness of the adult mammary gland varies with the individual, depending upon conditions and the accumulation of fat, the average being two inches. The nipple is located in the fourth interspace usually and its circular area of pigmented skin, the areola, is pinkish red, turning dark red during and after childbirth.

I bought the book and continued on my walk.

The Frick Museum faced Fifth Avenue and Central Park. The public entrance to the museum was on Seventieth Street. Above the entrance was a stone pediment by the American Sculptor Sherry E. Fry. It depicted a naked woman with a child on the knee of her extended leg. I arrived at the museum a quarter of an hour early and stood looking up at the mother and child for a few minutes before I crossed Fifth Avenue to gain a clear view of the building's facade. Its total effect, I admitted to myself, was of restrained but superlative grandeur. It was a distinctly European building and reflected architectural history from the period of Louis XVI through to the continental style of late nineteenth century France. Was this building, this palatial house, the pedigree of a new, North American aristocracy, a vigorous revival of tradition? Or was it a foible, a grand folly, a ritual farewell to a dying era, finally solemnised by the flow of traffic down Fifth Avenue; the buses, limousines, trucks and yellow cabs continually passing and blowing their exhaust into the Mansion's gardens?

Visitors to the Frick bought their tickets at an office window just inside and to the left of the building entrance. A guard in a maroon uniform then directed them to the cloakroom, after which they returned to the foyer, deposited their tickets in a box and entered the gallery through a turnstile.

I followed this procedure as far as the cloakroom but then sidetracked to the museum shop, in search of the biography. There appeared to be no one in the room. I glanced around impatiently and then looked out into the corridor. No, there was no one. I walked across to the bookshelves and immediately found what I wanted. It was a hard-covered book:

Henry Clay Frick
The Man
by
George Harvey

Taking a copy with me to the counter to wait I heard a noise. I leant forward and discovered a young, blonde woman crouched behind the counter at an open drawer of photographic slides. She leapt up, obviously disconcerted.

'Can I help you?' She appeared to be dizzy from getting up too quickly.

'Yes, please. May I buy this?'

The book proved to be only two or three dollars. Miss Frick, it seemed, was subsidising the public's access to the memory of her father.

'Is this the only biography written?'

'On Mr Frick?'

'Yes.'

'I think so, but you'd have to ask the curatorial staff. Would you like me to find out?'

She made a telephone call. I found myself studying her hair, which was loosely curled and still slightly damp. I speculatively imagined New York's working population showering in the morning, hurrying or lingering, millions of shower stalls veiled in steam, towels and nightwear dropped on tiled floors.

'Yes, sir, this is the only one.'

'Thank you, I appreciate that. No, there's no need to wrap it.'

'You know, you have a cute accent.'

It was my turn for embarrassment. I was not yet quite used to New Yorkers' readiness for blunt comment, open compliment.

Inside the gallery I stopped in the central courtyard and sat down on a bench overlooking the pool. I wanted at least a quick impression of the book. It was first published in 1936, privately. The table of contents included chapter headings like 'A triumph of Faith and Courage'. There was also a chapter titled 'Homestead' and another, 'Attempted Assassination'. This could be promising. I turned to the last chapter, 'Personality'.

> Mr Frick's most splendid inheritance from a long line of outdoor-bred ancestors was an exceptionally rugged constitution and, when he had mastered for the time the congenital infirmities of youth, he grew to be a powerful man physically.

The style was distracting but surely I would find some information somewhere here. I glanced several paragraphs ahead.

> His habits were methodical, punctuated by frequent manifestations of impatience at unnecessary interruption of routine; and he was never idle for a moment, nor even still except at such times as when, having finished the morning's dictation, he would thrust

his hands into his trousers' pockets, lean far back in his chair, half close his eyes and engage in the silent meditation allotted for the day; only to flash into action at its close in putting the determination reached summarily into effect. Even while holding this favorite posture of apparent repose, he personified power – under restraint.

I shut the book and sat watching the people passing through the courtyard. Their clothing looked misplaced in this setting, as though hurriedly borrowed from another era. The water fell so languidly from the fountain. A faint, musty humidity rose from the garden beds. The sound of voices came clearly from the foyer but here people spoke in whispers.

I walked through the museum looking at it as an extension of Frick's character; the decorative plasterwork of the building's interior, the marble, the great quantity of exposed stonework, the cabinets still full of books in what had been the library, the pipe organ on the landing of the main stairway. Frick had lived in this place, if only for a few years. He had walked through these rooms after dinner, had paused before the Rembrandt self-portrait in the West Gallery. What had he seen in this painting, in this painter with whom he would have gladly changed places? Certainly it is an extraordinary painting. It depicts the artist at fifty-two, nine years before his death. By this time Rembrandt had been forced to auction his house and possessions, including his art collection, which held paintings apparently by many of the masters of the Italian Renaissance. But he chose to portray himself in majestic pose, a cane resting in his hand like a sceptre.

'This painting was Mr Frick's favourite.'

I looked around startled. A guard, young and frizzy haired, was standing near me. He had spoken with authority, as though he had known the man himself.

'You were looking at the picture so long I thought you'd be interested to know.'

'Yes I am, thank you.'

He directed me to another painting, the Bellini *St Francis*, which he said Frick used to spend hours studying. I knew the *St Francis* through reproductions and had been looking forward to it already. On my way I paused in front of the Ingres portrait of Madame d'Haussonville.

It has been suggested that in Ingres's portraits the clothes wear the sitter. His grandfather had been the master tailor of Toulouse. Indeed when Ingres, who resisted particular portrait commissions for decades, did decide to paint someone, there followed interminable discussion about what should be worn. With this painting I had to admit there was a sumptuous presence, of cloth certainly, but also of Madame d'Haussonville. A friend of the sitter, Monsieur Thiers, on first seeing the portrait had declared: '*Il faut que Ingres soit amoureux de vous pour avoir peint ainsi.*' Ingres must have loved you to have painted you this way. What had Frick seen in this woman?

I caught the downtown subway before afternoon rush-hour and was lucky enough to find a seat. Now I had to admit I was intrigued by Frick himself. Logically he seemed to be a perfect representative of his time; a force in the development of his nation who didn't vacillate about the niceties of humanism. Every expansive culture depended on this sort of blind faith. Politically I could pigeonhole him, even if he seemed more resolute than most. But there was something here beyond historical or political relevance; something which didn't connect with my expectations. When I faced it I just couldn't accept that the Rembrandt self-portrait was his favourite painting. It was as though he didn't have the right to appreciate that picture. I had to laugh at myself. But the collection was generally so good, and had the stamp of individual discrimination. What sort of person was this? I sat on the train thinking. What would the encounter with Berkman, this clash which symbolised the fundamental dichotomy in politics for over a century, reveal about Frick? I opened the biography at chapter ten, 'Attempted Assassination'.

Alexander Berkman was a professed anarchist – a violent and destructive opponent of all goverment – and a disciple of the notorious Emma Goldman. He was born in the province of Vilna, Russia, in 1867, the son of a prosperous druggist, and while attending a college exploited views of such radical nature that he was expelled from the town by the authorities. He came to New York when nineteen . . .

Shouting. A man was shouting at the end of the subway car. He was black, probably in his early thirties. In fact, as I glanced around quickly I realised I was the only white person in the train. He came lurching down the aisle and stopped virtually in front of me. His eyes moved about distractedly.

'If you don't wanna see some crime, put some money here, now!' He held out his cap, his chin raised so that he looked down at his unwilling audience over tear-stained cheeks. As I reached forward with some coins he turned away.

'I don't understand you fuckin' people.'

He turned back and I succeeded in dropping the coins in his hat. He instantly reached in, took out some money, which I assumed was mine, or at least meant to be mine, and threw it down the length of the car.

'I don't understand you fuckin' people,' he shouted again. 'I ain't gonna stand this much longer. I don't give a damn if I die tomorrow but I can tell you this, I'm gonna take somebody with me.'

TWENTY-ONE
FAMILY ALBUM 2

'Have you done any cooking at all?'

'Not much. Both my parents are great cooks but I've avoided instruction.'

Elizabeth shook her head.

'I'm sorry.'

'Don't apologise. At least we know where to start.'

Elizabeth had offered to show me how to make corn bread. I had admired it the previous night, at dinner. Now I stood with her in the kitchen, her absolute domain.

'I feel totally incompetent.'

'As Steve says, you can't call yourself a man of culture unless you're capable in the kitchen.'

'Have you heard of Piero di Cosimo, the Italian Renaissance painter? He was afraid of fire. Every few weeks he'd summon the courage to light his stove and boil several dozen eggs. He'd live off them as long as possible. I'm afraid he's my sort of cultured man.'

'That's no excuse. Steven is terrified of fire and he's a great cook.'

'Steven Redman?'

'Yes, Steve. He'd love a gas stove but knows he'd be afraid to light it; so he makes do with electricity.'

'I don't believe you.'

'It's true. Steve is wracked with phobias. He always sits at the back of movie theatres, on the aisle, for fear of being burnt alive. He's scared of the winter cold, too; haven't you noticed how many scarves he wears?'

When I thought of it I did realise I had been fascinated by the minor spectacle of Steven wrapping himself in layers before stepping outdoors.

'We'll start with basics. Have you ever sautéed an onion?'

'No.'

'Don't look so worried. It's one of the basic activities in cooking.' Elizabeth pushed a wooden cutting board in front of me and placed a large onion and a knife on it. I peeled the onion, feeling clumsy, and began chopping at it with the knife. Elizabeth was busily criss-crossing the kitchen gathering ingredients.

'You'll use my big skillet.'

'Your what?' I said, turning towards her.

'My skillet.' She was holding up what I would have called a frying pan. 'What's the matter? Oh, I see, it's only the tragedy of the peeled onion.' She had noticed the tears on my cheeks.

Throughout this conversation I was keenly aware of Elizabeth's presence, a contained, bustling confidence in this her perfect setting. She was a small woman and delicately formed, but here she suggested physical solidity.

'Chop the thing, don't mutilate it.' She came forward and clasped my cutting hand in hers and firmly directed its movement. She leant lightly against me.

'Hi, honey.' Moishe had walked in through the kitchen door. Elizabeth sheered away from my side and greeted him with a kiss.

'How was your day?' she asked.

'Fine, but no orgasms. How about you my liebeh, any orgasms?'

'No, mine was a day sadly free from the little death.'

This banter was not unusual but today I was made slightly uncomfortable by it.

'And so, my Aussie mate, she's finally pressed you into

culinary service.' Moishe said this while hanging his coat on the back of a kitchen chair.

'I've rarely felt so incompetent.'

'Elizabeth will knock you into shape in no time.'

Moishe got himself a beer from the refrigerator and sat down at the table.

'Clarence Cohen asked me today how your research is going. I told him you were hard at work.'

I looked around at Moishe feeling less than sure of this myself.

'Did you get the biography yet?'

'Yes, yesterday.'

'Will it prove useful?'

'I think so. George Harvey's writing style is something in itself.' I quoted him, from memory, the line about Frick's outdoor-bred ancestors.

Moishe laughed.

'I picture Mr Frick's progenitors screwing in the undergrowth. You know, I was only thinking the other day how my experience of Australia changed screwing for me forever.'

Elizabeth and I both looked at him.

'Well, perhaps not literally, but the word. You use so many words for it: fucking, banging and knocking, poking, scraping and rooting and God knows how many more. It was rooting that made me an alien at home. Whenever people discuss their roots, or rooting for the "Knicks", I realise Australia changed me.' He paused to drink. 'But you're like your father, an unlikely Australian, you never fucking swear.'

'Only in anger,' I said apologetically.

'Now there's a subject; how people invoke copulation at their angriest. Go fuck this, go fuck that. Why use our finest sensory pleasure to damn our enemies? We don't tell them to "Go eat", or "Go take a hot shower", or send them to other lesser delights. I guess we're just fucked up.'

Elizabeth had poured a little olive oil into the frying pan, or skillet, and explained to me how the onion pieces are stirred, with a wooden spoon, over a low heat until translucent and turning golden. I watched them closely.

'Moishe,' I said, 'I discovered Miss Frick's name is Helen.'

'So?' He had opened the *New York Times* on the table.

'I seem to remember you thought her name embodied some Victorian virtue.'

'No, not at all.'

I was mildly disappointed by this exchange, not because of the petty misunderstanding but because Moishe's tone was dismissive, almost arrogant.

'Hi, everyone.' Ruth had rushed into the room. She was carrying her picture album. 'I have new things to show you all; you especially,' she said, staring at me with demanding eyes.

I finished the onions and joined the others at the table. Ruth turned back a page so I wouldn't miss anything.

'These are my pets.' She had cut out photographs of cats and dogs from every available source, snipping along their outlines and gluing them down in settings she had drawn with coloured pencils. There was a dog jumping over a garden; a cat lay on a tree branch; another dog swam in a pool, its body visible through the blue lines of drawn water. I was reminded of early Christian mosaics of Christ being baptised by St John. Standing in the river Jordan, Christ's legs are made to disappear into the water by shimmering lines of blue and green.

'Dad, when can we get a real dog?'

'We're not going to start this conversation again.'

'Why can't we have one?'

'I've told you before, who do you think would end up feeding the thing, taking it for walks and collecting its dooty from the streets?'

'Hannah and me would do it.'

'Hannah and I,' Moishe corrected.

'If you like, but I'm willing to help.'

'This is impossible,' said Moishe, his voice rising. He turned to me in mock despair. 'Have you considered the evolutionary genius of cats and dogs? What better strategy for survival could any species employ than to attach itself to the hearts of human children?'

Ruth, sensing that this avenue of attack was useless for the moment, turned the next couple of pages of animals and arrived, to my astonishment, at a double page of photographs of me.

'See,' she said looking at me, 'Hannah gave me all these.'

'I had no idea she'd taken so many.'

There was a photograph of me giving Herman a piggyback in the street. There was another of me lying in bed looking up over a book, with Ruth and Herman standing beside the bed holding pool cues. There were several of me at the dinner table and around the house. And there was one of Elizabeth and me, walking in the Japanese garden at the Brooklyn Botanical Gardens.

'You two make a handsome couple.' Moishe said this without a hint of irony.

'Aren't they cute,' added Ruth. 'Look at him here.' She pointed at a photo of me looking tired, leaning on my elbows at the table, after dinner. 'What a cute guy!'

Just as my discomfort with this situation was becoming acute, there was a flash of bright light. We all looked up. Hannah was standing in the doorway with her camera.

TWENTY-TWO
ATTEMPTED ASSASSINATION 2

According to George Harvey, Alexander Berkman obtained an interview with Frick for Saturday the twenty-third of July in the guise of the representative of an employment agency. The week before he had investigated the office.

If Berkman had gone prepared on that occasion, when he arrived about half past one and found his quarry absolutely alone, unsuspecting and helpless in his desk chair, he could have killed him with surety and ease.

Apparently affected by nervous tension, Berkman visited the company office twice on the Friday but found his way blocked by other callers.

At noon on Saturday he appeared a third time; but, when word came that Mr. Frick would be unable to see him for a few moments, he became so agitated that he left hurriedly and, apparently failing to calm his nerves sooner, did not return till nearly two o'clock, twenty minutes too late to find his victim alone. But this time he gave himself no opportunity to falter. Revolver in hand though still in his pocket, he brushed past the office boy, threw open the door and darted into the room drawing his weapon.

Frick was at his desk talking with Mr Leishman, his vice-chairman. The first shot was fired as he rose and turned towards the door. The bullet 'pierced the lobe of his left ear, entered his neck near the base of the skull and passed down between his shoulders.' As he toppled the second bullet entered the right side of his neck.

Mr Leishman leapt at Berkman, striking his hand up so that the third shot discharged into the ceiling. While they grappled, Frick, although bleeding badly, got to his feet and flung himself around Berkman's waist, knocking all three of them to the floor. Berkman wrenched his left hand free and, pulling from his pocket a dagger made from a file, stabbed Frick first in the hip, then in his right side and finally in the left leg below the knee. Despite this Frick managed to pin his assailant to the floor until help arrived and Berkman was overpowered.

But the nihilist had not yet reached the end of his resources. He was still struggling when a Deputy Sheriff, greatly excited, rushed into the room and was trying to get a clear shot at him without imperilling others when Mr. Frick, who had been leaning on his desk and watching keenly, made a gesture of dissuasion.

'Don't shoot,' he ejaculated, 'leave him to the law; but raise his head and let me see his face.'

This demand having been complied with none too gently, the sheriff, following the direction indicated by Mr. Frick's index finger, saw the culprit's jaw moving as if he were chewing something. Instantly his mouth was forced open and a capsule containing enough fulminite of mercury to blow all in the room to bits was extracted. This was too much for a carpenter who, having rushed in from his work hammer in hand, struck at, but missed, Berkman's head and was drawing back for another blow when again Mr. Frick interceded faintly:

'Don't kill him, I tell you; let the law take its course.'

While Frick was having his wounds staunched, lying on a couch, he had a message sent to his wife and also dictated two telegrams. The first was to his mother: 'Was shot twice but not dangerously. H.C. Frick.' The second was to Carnegie:

'There is no necessity for you to come home. I am still in shape to fight the battle out.'

He then, after refusing anaesthetic, assisted the doctor who probed for the bullets lodged in his body:

> . . . the surgeon inserted the instrument and pushed it forward gently and tentatively in pursuance of the patient's directions until in each of the two searches he heard 'There, that feels like it, Doctor,' and extracted both balls with unerring precision.

Frick then completed the day's work before being carried to an ambulance and taken home. Before leaving the office he issued a statement to the press:

> This incident will not change the attitude of the Carnegie Steel Company towards the Amalgamated Association. I do not think I shall die but whether I do or not the Company will pursue the same policy and it will win.

For the next ten days he worked from bed, continuing to control the company's response to the strike. On the fifth of August he returned to his office, travelling in an open street car.

> 'Those who hate him most,' wrote the correspondent of the *New York World*, his severest critic, 'admire the nerve and stamina of this man of steel whom nothing seems able to move. He looked a little thinner and paler than before he was shot but the change was not so marked as had been expected. There is a mark on his left ear where a bullet passed through it and behind the ear is a hole stuffed with cotton in which the bullet buried itself. He was particularly interested in the hole in the ceiling made by the bullet when Mr. Leishman knocked up Berkman's arm and which, but for that act, would have ended his career. But he was not worried when he was attacked nor while lying in his home during those terribly hot days when his recovery was anything but certain, and today, when he

returned to work after thirteen days, he seemed just the same as ever. There was no bodyguard.'

'If an honest American,' he remarked to the *Times* reporter, 'cannot live in his own home without being surrounded by a body guard, it is time to quit.'

The *World* correspondent asked how he was feeling.

'Very well, indeed, thank you,' answered Mr. Frick. 'I am nearly well, and in very good trim for work. I had too much to do to stay away from the office any longer and I am glad to get back again. I am going right along now attending to my affairs. Fortunately there is nothing behind, for during my absence the work has been done most satisfactorily by the officials and clerks. I could not ask any better management of this trouble than that of my assistants, and the results thus far are all that could be wished for. There have been many grave situations and complications and all of them have been sucessfully met. The outlook is most bright. I could not ask for anything better.'

Henry Clay Frick the second had been born on the day of the battle at Homestead. He died less than four weeks later, two days before his father returned to the office after his forced convalescence.

After twelve years, movements both for and against the early release of Alexander Berkman appealed to Frick for support. He refused all requests, 'upon his own tenet to the affect that, once the law was invoked in any matter, no species of influence should be brought to bear upon the courts in their dispensation of justice.'

When news of Frick's death, on the second of December 1919, reached Berkman he remarked, 'Well anyhow he left the country before I did.' Later that same day Berkman and Emma Goldman were deported by the United States Government.

TWENTY-THREE
REVIVAL HOUSE

The night was dark but the massive span of the Verrazano Bridge, stretching away above us and to our left, was darker. Without moonlight the water looked flat and cold. We were on the Belt Parkway travelling towards Manhattan. The car was moving quickly; Steven, who was driving, enjoyed speed. I leant forward in the seat looking out the window, and thought of the wheels turning on the surface of the road beneath us.

With the advent of the automobile Frick came to adore speed, until traffic regulations began to frustrate him. He hired a chauffeur from France, the most daring and experienced he could find, who flaunted the law of the road. But eventually, with the mass-production of cars, traffic jams thwarted his pleasure and caused him to abandon motoring as a pastime.

The others in the car were talking. I heard Moishe's voice vibrating beside me in the back seat. Natalie was beside him at the other window and Elizabeth was in the front with Steven. Without listening to what they were saying the essential Americanness of their voices filtered through to me. I concentrated on the moving view of the night and the thud of the wheels as they hit seams in the bitumen.

Lights began to increase across the harbour on the New Jersey shore and in clusters on the water.

'Is that the Statue of Liberty?'

'Surely,' answered Natalie.

'The symbol of the land of the free,' said Steven. I had previously noticed, with interest, his tendency for political cynicism.

'Don't start your anti-American spiel,' retorted Natalie.

In the distance the statue was vaguely defined by the light of her torch.

'Let's shift from democracy to demography. Can you see Ellis Island?' Moishe pointed out to me a lump just distinguishable from its surrounding water and speckled with a few lights. 'Between 1891 and 1954 Ellis Island was the clearing house for twenty million migrants, the official doorway to this country, the witness to our polyglot society. Before that it was an arsenal and a fort.'

'And earlier this century it was also the clearing house for thousands of political prisoners on their way to deportation by the United States government.' Steven's tone was abrupt. No one took the conversation further.

I could now see the southern tip of Manhattan from my window. There was absolutely no mistaking it. It was not important that I had inevitably seen a myriad photographs of this island, countless backdrops to advertisements and films. The view of the city from Steven's speeding car was acting on me like some primordial locus. The multi-faceted collection of skyscrapers in the business district was transformed by countless lights into a monumental fairyland. It was a grand folly, an architectural Disneyland made truly spectacular by the flatness of the island and the height of the lit-up towers, which seemed to rise directly from the water. I thought of the Dean and Chapter of Seville who in 1401 declared that a church would be built of such greatness that succeeding generations would think them mad even to have attempted it. Five hundred and eighty years later, on another continent, the motivation was no longer the glorification of God. The formative impulse here was commercial but surely the result was no less insane.

Earlier that day I walked from the college library to Moishe's office. There was no wind and the green tips of the trees suggested that winter was truly over. In the courtyard there was silence, for the first time since my arrival. I peered down into the pit suspiciously. The machine was still there but a man in a blue plastic suit was moving the pipes that ran from it. He looked up at me.

'Howdy,' he called.

In the office Moishe and Steven were sitting talking. It had been pre-arranged that I would meet them, we would collect Elizabeth and Natalie in Brooklyn and drive to the city, see a movie and eat out. Moishe poured me a cup of coffee. I looked at my watch.

'There's no hurry,' he said. 'Relax, drink up!'

I took the cup. Moishe never remembered that I rarely drank coffee. It had a disproportionately strong effect on me. He would force cup after cup into my hand and I would drink them, somehow caught up in the ritual of conversation and coffee.

'I was just telling Steve about my grandmother. She had this thing for toilet brushes. She used to set fire to them. When I was a kid she lived with us. Every few months she'd appear in the kitchen holding a smouldering toilet brush, in a state of complete confusion. The rest of the time her behaviour was pretty regular. She finally locked herself in the bathroom a few years ago and by the time my dad broke in the door the room was full of smoke, and she was sitting on the toilet, dead.'

Already I could feel myself being overtaken by a slight sense of unreality. I knew I had heard something like this before. It teased me. And I couldn't tell whether Moishe found the story about his grandmother amusing or tragic, or both.

'I knew this guy,' said Steven, 'who climbed into his refrigerator with several dozen twinkies and a couple of bottles of scotch. He was missing for days. People searched his apartment a few times for clues before someone opened the fridge.'

'That was a kind of thoughtful way to commit suicide,' commented Moishe. 'At least he wouldn't have decomposed, huh?'

'What are "twinkies"?' I asked, fixating in my caffeine-affected state.

'They're a sort of junk-food cake.'

By the time we parked near the movie theatre I felt almost normal. Steve had had to cruise around several blocks and finally, in what I had discovered was another New York custom, had 'bunted' the car in front of him so he could fit into the only space he could find.

As we walked along the sidewalk Moishe took me by the arm.

'You are about to experience your first visit to a New York revival house, an important development in any human being's education.'

'Do you remember that the term revival house has another meaning in Australia?' I asked.

'No, I don't think so.'

'It's an establishment for the reawakening of Christian fervour.'

Moishe laughed.

'Of course, I should have remembered. They have revival meetings here too, but you know I don't care much for Christianity.' He paused and glanced at me. 'For that matter I'm not much interested in my own religion. Being Jewish is a matter of cultural identity and I go along with the religious customs only that far. But I like this twin notion of religious fervour and old movies. Perhaps we should call these places movie-fervour-houses. Hey, honey!' he yelled out to Elizabeth who was walking behind with Steven and Natalie. 'We're going to the movie-fervour-house!'

'What are you talking about?' she shouted back.

The theatre was quite small. Paint was peeling off the walls and ceiling, the floor was littered with Coke cups and paper, and there was a faint musty smell. Elizabeth had been right; Steve insisted on sitting at the back of the theatre on the aisle. As we took our seats I smiled at Elizabeth and she reached out and clasped my hand briefly. The film opened with a B52 bomber being refuelled in midair. The two aircraft swayed, and rose and fell delicately on the air-currents as the titles rolled past. The movie was Stanley Kubrick's *Dr. Strangelove*.

'Well, what did you think?' asked Steve of everyone, as he sprinkled dried chilli on his pizza.

'Too many airplanes for me. I don't like movies with all these airplanes,' said Moishe.

'Can't you be serious?'

'Seriously, I didn't like it. It's a negative movie.'

'Fine Moishe, the film is about the destruction of the earth by nuclear radiation and you want it to be positive.'

'Well, I think it's defeatist and basically anti-human. Kubrick obviously couldn't give a shit for people.'

'Have you heard of satire?'

'I don't call Vera Lynn singing "We'll meet again, don't know where, don't know when" while the bombs explode satire. I call it puerile posturing.'

'But that was fantastic. It's the apposition of such opposites that shocks people into understanding something.'

'Shocks who? The converted feel smugly indignant and the unconverted tune it all out.'

'The movie made me tense,' said Natalie.

'In Kubrick's view of things you're past tense.'

Moishe sat back in his chair unassailably calm.

'Well how in hell do you change anything?' Steve, in contrast, was unusually excited. He turned to me as he said this. 'How would you make that movie?'

Moishe leant forward, suddenly interested.

'Yes, you were born only a year or two before *Dr. Strangelove* was made. How does it affect you?'

Put on the spot so suddenly I dropped my slice of pizza and it landed upside-down on the table top. Everyone laughed with abandonment to the sort of communal hilarity, that, after the event, seems quite unsustainable. As usual, while listening to the conversation, I had been taking in my surroundings. This was only another pizza place to these New Yorkers but to me everything had yet to be positioned on a still very fluid scale of cultural equivalents. On each table was pepper and salt, chilli, tomato sauce or rather ketchup, and mild American mustard. The floor was covered with white tiles, here and there spotted with dropped chewing gum. Mirrors ran around the walls just above table height, revealing unexpected views of the other customers. Outside, on the Avenue of the Americas, the traffic stopped and started at a set of lights in a persistent rhythm.

'Come on,' said Moishe. 'You can't divert us that easily.'

'Kubrick must have done something successfully; the film attracted enough attention.'

Everyone was looking at me, waiting.

'That's too glib an answer? Alright. I suppose I'd have made the film differently. Parts of it annoyed me formally. But I tend to stress formal considerations in everything. As for subject matter, I probably do sympathise with Kubrick's disillusionment with human intelligence when it comes to the big issues. Do you bother to do anything about a prospect like nuclear war and if so what? Kubrick decided to make a bleakly satirical film. You know I've been reading about Alexander Berkman, the anarchist who shot Frick. He disapproved of a society fundamentally based on greed. He decided to kill an eminent and ruthless industrialist as a contribution to change.'

'But that's murder.' Natalie was outraged.

'He actually claimed to have nothing against Frick personally. He considered him no less a human being than anyone else, but he shot him as a symbol of power, wealth and injustice.'

'That must be great,' said Moishe, 'being dead without it meaning anything personal.'

'This is crazy.' Natalie glared at me.

'Well, I suppose you could establish a pretty compelling case that Berkman's act was extreme. But was it more extreme than Frick's business practices?'

'Here we come down to discussing political values, and you can count me out,' said Moishe.

Going home, as we drove downtown, I felt as though we were sliding down a long hill; the lights of Broadway were like grease lubricating our departure. It was late and even the theatre traffic had thinned. As we approached the Brooklyn Bridge I turned around in my seat to watch the city loom up and recede behind us. There it was in light-spangled glory, this monument to the new world, this fantasy of concrete, steel and glass. I felt extraordinarily, romantically indulgent towards the city. And I was glad that I would have a memory of it in this mood.

TWENTY-FOUR
ATTEMPTED ASSASSINATION 3

'Extra large steak! Extra cup of coffee!'

These were the first words that Emma Goldman heard Alexander Berkman say. It was Goldman's first day in New York, the fifteenth of August 1889. She had been taken to Sachs' café on Suffolk Street, the favourite gathering place for radicals on the East Side.

'Who is that glutton?' she asked her companion.

'That is Alexander Berkman. He can eat for three. But he rarely has enough money for much food. When he has he eats Sachs out of his supplies. I'll introduce you to him.'

In this way began a relationship which continued for over forty years, despite interruption.

He was no more than a boy, hardly eighteen, but with the neck and chest of a giant. His jaw was strong, made more pronounced by his thick lips. His face was almost severe, but for his high, studious forehead and intelligent eyes. A determined youngster, I thought.

So Emma Goldman described Berkman in her autobiography.

In May 1892 Berkman, Goldman and a friend, Fedya, were running an ice-cream parlour, in Worcester, Massachusetts. This strangely *petit bourgeois* activity had been undertaken to raise money for their return to Russia, their homeland, to take part in revolutionary activity there. News of the Homestead confrontation suggested that the American worker had become 'determined to break the chains that held him in bondage so long'. The three friends became preoccupied with Homestead. They served ice-cream and fried pancakes by day but stayed up late into the nights discussing the strike.

One afternoon a customer came in for an ice-cream, while I was alone in the store. As I set the dish down before him, I caught the large headlines of his paper: 'LATEST DEVELOPMENTS IN HOMESTEAD – FAMILIES OF STRIKERS EVICTED FROM THE COMPANY HOUSES – WOMAN IN CONFINEMENT CARRIED OUT INTO STREET BY SHERIFFS.' I read over the man's shoulder Frick's dictum to the workers: he would rather see them dead than concede to their demands, and he threatened to import Pinkerton detectives. The brutal bluntness of the account, the inhumanity of Frick towards the evicted mother, inflamed my mind. Indignation swept my whole being. I heard the man at the table ask: 'Are you sick, young lady? Can I do anything for you?' 'Yes, you can let me have your paper,' I blurted out. 'You won't have to pay for the ice-cream. But I must ask you to leave. I must close the store.' The man looked at me as if I had gone crazy.

The same day they abandoned the ice-cream parlour. Leaving with the day's takings they returned to New York to prepare a manifesto for the steel workers.

A few days after our return to New York the news flashed across the country of the slaughter of steel workers by Pinkertons.

The wanton murders aroused even the daily papers. Several came out in strong editorials, severely criticizing Frick. He had gone too far; he had added fuel to the fire in the labour ranks and would have himself to blame for any desperate acts that might come.

We were stunned. We saw at once that the time for our manifesto had passed. Words had lost their meaning in the face of the innocent blood spilled on the banks of the Monongahela. Intuitively each felt what was surging in the heart of the others. Sasha broke the silence. 'Frick is the responsible factor in this crime,' he said; 'he must be made to stand the consequences.' It was the psychological moment for an 'Attentat'; the whole country was aroused, everybody was considering Frick the perpetrator of a cold blooded murder. A blow aimed at Frick would re-echo in the poorest hovel, would call the attention of the whole world to the real cause behind the Homestead struggle. It would strike terror in the enemy's ranks and make them realise that the proletariat of America had its avengers.

Berkman worked at night over the next week in the feverish July heat, spending much of the friends' money, attempting to build two bombs. He took one of them to Staten Island to test it but returned home dejected; the bomb had failed to explode.

There remained only fifteen dollars; enough to take Berkman to Pittsburgh and keep him for a day but not enough to buy a gun. He went ahead, leaving Goldman to raise twenty dollars. Unable to think of another solution she decided to prostitute herself. A sixty-year-old man picked her up on the street and took her to a bar.

He only wanted to tell me that there was nothing in prostitution unless one had the knack for it. 'You haven't got it, that's all there is to it,' he assured me. He took out a ten dollar bill and put it down before me. 'Take this and go home,' he said.

The rest of the money Goldman borrowed from her impoverished sister.

Early in the afternoon of Saturday, the twenty-third of July, Goldman, who had been waiting in a state of extreme tension, read the first headline: 'YOUNG MAN BY THE NAME OF ALEXANDER BERGMAN SHOOTS FRICK – ASSASSIN OVERPOWERED BY WORKING-MEN AFTER DESPERATE STRUGGLE.' She bought all the afternoon newspapers.

Everyone had a different description but the main fact stood out – our brave Sasha had committed the act! Frick was still alive, but his wounds were considered fatal. He would probably not survive the night. And Sasha – they would kill him. They were going to kill him I was sure of it.

TWENTY-FIVE
NINE TIMES THREE

Hannah was the last to come downstairs. Over her pyjamas she was wearing her grey dressing-gown, carefully chosen to co-ordinate with the colour of her bedroom walls. On her feet were striped socks, multi-pastel coloured, like Italian ice-cream. Her hair was tousled and the rich skin of her face still had the texture of sleep, of being pressed against the polyester-cotton blend of her pillow-case.

It was Sunday morning. Everyone had slept in until ten or eleven, except for Elizabeth, who had got up early and cycled to the nearest shops to buy pastries and bring home the forest-destroying bulk of the Sunday *New York Times*. She also had cooking to do, for that morning was to be a time of family self-indulgence, of orchestrated excess.

The members of the family rose in stages, roused by sumptuous odours from the kitchen and lured downstairs from bed. We had to wait to eat until everything was prepared. At eleven-thirty Steven and Natalie arrived, both wearing tracksuit bottoms and tee-shirts, both feisty from their morning jog in the spring air.

'Herman, go wake Hannah!' yelled Moishe from the living-room, where he had just put on a Miles Davis record. Moishe had explained to me the importance of Miles Davis. I could now recognise the sound of his trumpet. That morning there had been prolonged negotiations between Moishe and Ruth over control of the record player. Moishe, under great pressure, had yielded to one side of 'The Clash' but only after both sides of Miles Davis had been played. Herman put in an unsuccessful bid for one of his recordings of the Muppets.

As Hannah arrived everyone jostled into the kitchen, gathering around the table. The blue and white checked tablecloth was barely visible beneath the plates and bowls of food. There was, of course, a basket of bagels and cream cheese on a plate. There were pastries and rolls in another basket. Elizabeth had made waffles. There was a jug of maple syrup and a bowl of strawberry jam. She had also cooked 'blintzes', Jewish pancakes filled with cottage cheese or blueberries. She had baked apple cake and honey cake and also made noodle kugel, a creamy pudding studded with raisins. There was coffee and hot chocolate; there was rye bread and pumpernickel.

'How's our resident anarchist this morning?' Natalie asked when we were seated and food was being passed back and forth along the table.

'In pretty good order, thank you.' I smiled at her across the table.

'You know, Natalie, just reading a book about Alexander Berkman doesn't make you an anarchist,' said Moishe.

'Really, Moishe? I didn't realise.'

'What's an anarchist?' asked Ruth.

'A person who eats babies and rapes old ladies,' suggested Steven.

Ruth looked at me and grinned.

‘Anarchy is chaos,’ said Natalie defiantly.

‘Actually,’ corrected Steven, ‘anarchism was developed as a political philosophy. Its tenets were the repudiation of centralised government and the voluntary association and co-operation of individuals.’

‘That sounds like chaos to me,’ said Moishe.

‘Have you ever considered how weird it is when people shake hands?’ Hannah said this quietly, to no one in particular, but brought immediate silence to the table. ‘You face each other, put out your right hand and your palms connect. Isn’t that amazing?’

‘There’s social organisation for you,’ said Steve, breaking Hannah’s spell over the conversation.

‘It’s funny you should say that, Hannah, because your great-grandmother couldn’t get shaking hands right.’ Moishe was unusually reflective. ‘She always put out her left hand, throwing the person she was meeting into confusion. She had her idiosyncracies, my grandmother. She always wore black to weddings; she thought they were occasions of great sadness. Even when she liked the bride and groom she cried.’

‘I remember one wedding with your grandmother crying,’ said Elizabeth. ‘There was a Chinese celebrant.’

‘Goddam it!’ cried Moishe, slapping his thighs. ‘That was some wedding! The bride and groom were Jewish but wanted absolutely no religious overtones to the ceremony. They hired a Chinese celebrant who turned up in full Mandarin costume. He called upon nature to bless the union. You could hear Grandmother sobbing in the background while the families and guests, all incredibly Jewish, stood with their mouths hanging open.’

While the conversation moved on through various weddings and marriages my concentration drifted to the table. I was unused to a feast of such sweetness. Was the basic life force of this culture sugar? I looked at Herman who was pouring syrup onto his waffle. The glistening liquid was dropping onto the waffle, running over its sides and pooling on the plate. Ruth was smearing thick gobs of strawberry jam onto a roll. Hannah was eating a blintz; blueberries squeezed from the end of the pancake as she applied pressure with her fork. I looked at Natalie, who sat directly opposite me. She was biting into a walnut pastry called 'rugelach'. Her fine white teeth reminded me of the smiling women from the world of television advertising. Altogether there was something of that commerical freshness about her body. Once again, I found myself looking at her breasts, which were distinct in their tee-shirt as usual. In the words of my newly found anatomy text, these must have been the conditions that promote the accumulation of fat in the adult mammary gland.

Glancing up I noticed Elizabeth was smiling at me from the end of the table. As though she had been able to read my thoughts I was briefly overcome with confusion. It occurred to me that I had never been distracted by Elizabeth's breasts. Why? Certainly, they were less obvious than Natalie's. Was Moishe correct? Was it merely the enhancement of Natalie's clothing that drew my attention?

'Alright everyone, I've got a riddle for you,' announced Hannah.

'OK,' said Moishe.

'Fire away,' added Steve.

'There are these three guys –'

'There are three guys, will do,' corrected Moishe.

'Who's telling the story?' Hannah glared at her father. 'There are these three guys who are travelling together. They stop at a hotel for the night. The man at the desk tells them it will cost thirty dollars for them to share a room. Each traveller pays his share, ten dollars, OK? The bellhop shows them to the room. The receptionist realises he made a mistake. There's this special price this week. The room is only twenty-five dollars. He gives the bellhop five dollars to take back to the guests. On his way upstairs the bellhop realises he can't divide five into three parts so he keeps two dollars and gives the men a dollar each. So, how much did each guest pay?'

'Nine dollars,' shouted Ruth.

'OK, nine dollars. Now, nine times three equals twenty seven, plus the two dollars the bellhop kept equals twenty nine dollars. What happened to the extra dollar?'

There was silence at the table.

'Wait a minute,' said Moishe. 'They ended up paying twenty-five dollars. The bellhop brought back five, three for the guests and two for himself. Twenty-five plus five equals thirty. There's no problem.'

'How much did each man end up paying?'

'Nine dollars, I suppose.'

'Nine times three is twenty-seven, plus two is twenty-nine. What happened to the dollar?'

'OK, OK, let me think.'

Again there was silence.

'This is ridiculous,' Moishe blurted out.

'Well, what's the answer?' asked Steven.

'Alright, I give up,' Moishe said reluctantly,

'There is no answer.'

'What do you mean there is no answer?' demanded Moishe.

'That's it, there's no answer. The dollar can't be explained.'

'This is mathematics we're talking about. Whole numbers don't just disappear.'

'This is beginning to appeal to me.' Steven was smiling broadly.

'Oh great. Throw logic out the window. We've lost the whole basis of civilised thought here!' Moishe's voice was getting louder.

'Yelling won't bring it back,' said Elizabeth.

'You have a child, you bring her up and look what happens. She brings the despair of the irrational into your home.'

'It's only one dollar, Dad,' said Ruth, reaching out to pat her father's hand from across the table. 'Can I put on The Clash now?'

TWENTY-SIX
YOUNG FRICK

On Frick's first day at school, at the age of eight, his teacher, Mr Voight, behaved in a way that was totally unpremeditated. Mr Voight bowed low to the boy and led him by the hand onto the stage at the front of the classroom.

'I present to you Mr Henry Clay Frick,' he said impressively.

Recalling the episode years later Mr Voight said he could only account for this introduction as a purely intuitive recognition of his most illustrious student.

Frick, in turn, behaved unusually. After a moment of abashed hesitation he bowed in imitation of his teacher, bringing cheers and laughter from the class.

This is one of a number of anecdotes George Harvey relates from Frick's boyhood.

Frick turned out to be an average student, except in one area. He excelled in mathematics. Before his teens he was considering his first million dollars: 'I propose to be worth that before I die.' His maternal grandfather, a whisky distiller, had assets valued at half a million dollars on his death. He provided his grandson with a model for achievement. At fifteen the boy refused to wear the clothes his family could provide. Despite the difficulty of earning enough money, he clothed himself.

At sixteen an uncle gave Frick a clerk's job in his general store. He proved to be an aggressive salesman, but it was bookkeeping that most appealed to him. He was assiduous in mastering the ornate calligraphy then used in accounting. While it appealed to him visually, the skill also improved his prospects in business. At the same time he became business manager of the literary society of his college. Among other activities he helped collect books to expand the library. He read a good deal, his favourite book being Abbott's admiring biography of Napoleon. His everyday name, Clay, he decided, lacked the necessary professional tone and he began referring to himself as Henry C. Frick and signing his name H. C. Frick.

Frick's career as a salesman progressed rapidly. He changed firms a couple of times with increased pay. He made himself popular with the customers, 'especially with the ladies'. This success caused some jealousy amongst his colleagues but he 'was so tactful and goodnatured that after a while he won all of them over and made them like him in spite of themselves.'

His routine was strict. He got up and dressed at seven, crossed the river on the way to the store:

> . . . arriving promptly at eight and remaining till six, returned to his boarding house for supper, recrossed the river to a business college, where he applied his mind sedulously to the study of accountancy and methods of banking till nine-thirty; then finally 'home' to his hall room and sleep.

After five months, typhoid fever sent Frick home to be nursed by his family. As he recovered his grandfather offered him the job of chief bookkeeper, on a thousand dollars a year, at the distillery. The manager was a cousin, Abraham Tintsman, and although he was about twice Frick's age the two quickly found a preoccupation in common: the potential for coke manufacture from local coal. Young Frick was convinced that coke would prove the cheapest and, in time, the essential fuel for the rapidly expanding steel mills of Pittsburgh. The two men, with two other partners, began buying plots of land. Frick borrowed money from the local farmers to finance his share of the business. His father, who had never gone into debt for himself, allowed Frick to borrow against everything he owned. His success in raising credit was unusual.

The partners, in a show of faith in the young man, agreed to call the new firm 'Frick & Co.', and gave him temporary management of its affairs. He immediately invested the entire capital of the business in low-priced land, leaving nothing for its development. He then attempted to finance the firm itself by credit. He went directly to Judge Thomas Mellon of the Mellon Bank in Pittsburgh. He wanted to borrow ten thousand dollars for six months at ten per cent interest, with which to build fifty coke ovens, upon security of undeveloped but unmortgaged coal lands.

It is more than doubtful that any other banker in Pittsburgh would have entertained the proposal for a moment, but Judge Mellon, the most cautious and conservative of them all, made the loan at once, without requiring endorsements, authorisation or corroboration of the young man's statements from his partners.

Admittedly Mellon did own coal lands throughout the region.

Before the fifty ovens were complete Frick requested another loan of ten thousand dollars for the building of fifty more. This time Mellon sent a representative to evaluate the enterprise. The report was unfavourable. The business was small, the responsible director, hardly more than a boy, was at the same time keeping the books for a large store and also collecting 'prints and sketches'. He worked from a 'half-office and half-living room in a clapboard shack'. Mellon was unconvinced and, perhaps impressed by Frick's frugality, sent a partner to make a second examination. The result won Frick his money.

Lands good, ovens well built; manager on the job all day, keeps books evenings, may be a little too enthusiastic about pictures but not enough to hurt; knows his business down to the ground; advise making the loan.

Frick & Co. built another fifty ovens and began to make a profit adequate to repay both loans to Mellon. But between 1873 and 1877 came an economic downturn which caused the collapse of the coke industry. The problem quickly became less one of producing coke at a loss than simply one of trying to dispose of it on any terms at all. Frick, virtually alone among producers, decided it was better to maintain his plant in operation than risk its deterioration. He would also be well placed to promptly fill orders when the industry eventually recovered. He became his own sales agent. Getting up at six, he oversaw the start of work, caught the train into Pittsburgh, travelled from factory to factory soliciting orders, and returned home to manage the mines until bedtime.

Despite the strictures of the situation Frick went on buying coal-bearing land. Although the land was cheap and the purchases could be financed largely by credit, part payment often had to be made. He found an unlikely solution. The little locally owned railway which carried Frick's coke to the main Baltimore-and-Ohio line was near bankruptcy through lack of traffic. He spent a long day gathering options from the shareholders. Next morning he presented the management of the Baltimore-and-Ohio with an offer to sell them the line at cost price. His scheme succeeded, along with a fifty thousand dollar commission for acting as negotiator and intermediary. A large part of the money he invested in further ovens and land.

There was another area where credit did not serve Frick's purpose. It could not provide his workmen's families with physical provisions. Here too he found a way round the problem. The company printed its own money and used it to pay the wages. At first the notes were spent at the company store but they rapidly became the common currency for the entire community. In this way Frick & Co. had use of all the income earnt from its coking business.

When Frick's grandmother died towards the end of 1874 his health faltered. According to Abraham Tintsman he 'never showed much of what he felt but he couldn't seem to smile and his eyes were very sad.' Worn out by constant work and the search for short-term expedients he spent six weeks in bed, seriously ill. When he returned to work, business was no better but the company's credit had remained unimpaired despite his absence.

It was not until early 1878 that the economic revival for which Frick had positioned himself began in earnest. The demand for steel, particularly for heavy railway track, suddenly became intense. The Pittsburgh mills found only one coke supplier prepared to meet their needs. They flocked to the Frick & Co. premises, 'where, at a plain desk in his modest office, calmly sat a sturdy, alert, keen eyed, soft spoken young man of few words but of amazing activities, no less surely than unpretentiously conscious of his complete mastery of the situation.' The price of coke rose from an unprofitable ninety cents to five dollars a ton.

Both production and construction were pushed to the very top notch of capacity; employés numbered nearly a thousand and car-loads shipped daily nearly a hundred before the year 1879 was ended.

On the evening of December 19th, his thirtieth birthday, Clay Frick dropped into the store on his way home from a prolonged game of chess following supper with his cousins, took a look at the books preliminary to the annual accounting, bought a fresh five-cent Havana cigar on credit, lighted it thoughtfully, strolled placidly around the corner . . . and went to bed.

He had made his million.

TWENTY-SEVEN
METROPOLITAN

I was leaning against a wall outside the entrance of the Metropolitan Museum of Art. At the foot of the broad steps in front of me there were, as usual, a couple of pretzel and hotdog vendors. Each trolley had a queue waiting to be served. A young woman near me was eating a pretzel, decorated with ribbons of livid yellow mustard. People sat on the steps in clusters; couples talking, absorbing the sunlight. It seemed quite crowded for a weekday afternoon. But there were always the tourists. What was it about this city that drew us all there? What substance fleshed out the myth? What made New York more desirable than anywhere else? New York was perhaps the most complete of monuments to human parochialism. Its flat topography, its grid layout, its three-dimensional concrete excesses, its conglomeration of races and types, its concentration on the preoccupations of business and entertainment; all these things combined to make the city a conceit of the imagination. Where else could one so easily forget everything except the activities of people? But what, in absolute terms, made New York more interesting than any other spot on earth?

I was waiting for Elizabeth. At breakfast we had arranged to meet outside the museum at two o'clock. It was now nearly half past two. I had spent the morning in the museum looking at paintings. I watched the traffic on Fifth Avenue. In a minute or two the same cars would be passing the Frick Museum.

There was was a constant flow of people on the Metropolitan

steps. I had noticed a tall man in a greatcoat hovering near the main entrance behind me. He watched the crowd eagerly. He followed people to the rubbish bins by the entrance and retrieved their soft drink cans and bottles, slipping them into a large bag. He saw me watching him and winked at me.

'Hey man,' he shouted out. 'You don't look local, you know, like New York. And you don't look like no regular tourist neither.' He walked over and looked at me, closely.

'I'm Australian.'

'Hey yeh! You from Sydney?'

'No, but I grew up there.'

'Can a man from Sydney spare a man from New York a dime?'

I gave him some change. He winked at me and started singing, a sort of jazz scat to the tune 'I Got Rhythm', as he wandered off to check the bins.

My attention turned back to the stairs. I scanned the moving figures for Elizabeth. For a moment I thought I saw her but it was another woman. I watched her climbing the steps, gauging the extent of my mistake. She was younger, more thickset than Elizabeth, but the short black hair and compact movements of her body were similar.

Asking a New Yorker to judge New York in absolute terms was like asking Moishe to buy a colour television. Rather, the absolute was judged in terms of New York. Steven had recently told me, without a trace of irony, that he never visited the country because there were bees there. I thought of my solo bushwalks in the south-eastern ranges of Australia. As a teenager I had loved to watch the timeless disorder of the forest: 'the architecture of chance', I had called it. In recent conversations with Moishe this idea had come up several times. My father had actually taken him on a walk and Moishe had been bemused by the experience. He liked to remember that.

'Through the history of civilised thought there's been an ongoing debate about the relative virtues of urban and rural life. You know the sort of thing: the concentration of people in the cities allows specialisation, a great diversiy of activities, of culture, of entertainment and the rest; but the country has clean air, fresh vegetables, clear-skinned young women and long siestas – in other words, nature. Both arms of the debate have their claim to romance. But your father took me to these incredible places! You talk about the architecture of chance. I'd call it the architecture of disorder, the desolation of elemental chaos. Everywhere there was wood, tangled wood and prickly things, and rocks and twigs and dead leaves. That was no place for people. But your father seemed at home there.'

I looked across Fifth Avenue at the well-kept facades of the apartment buildings. This was the upper East Side. Moishe had told me that here were possibly the wealthiest few square miles of human habitation on the planet. Yet, as I explored the city I saw clear signs of advanced decay, disintegration. I saw it nearly everywhere. How was the monolithic structure of the city to be maintained? It was so large, so complex that there were no longer enough resources available to stay the continuous, undermining process of physical entropy.

When Frick bought his block at Fifth Avenue and Seventieth Street, New York was already a big city, but most of the feats of its development had yet to come. The age of the skyscraper had yet to arrive.

When the Abstract Expressionists were painting, New York was at its zenith. Or perhaps its zenith had already begun to pass into mythology.

What sustained New York's mythology now? Weren't there other cities as big or bigger, and other cities with as much culture if not as much show business? Was New York a symbol? Did it epitomise the fast, vigorous materialism of the century? But what of Berlin, riding the knife edge between East and West; wasn't Berlin the true symbol of our age? Or Tokyo? Was it the *new* symbol, the centre of post-industrial economic power? But where was the romance there?

I watched the man in the greatcoat accost a pair of young

men who were standing at the top of the steps, drinking soda and smoking cigarettes.

'You guys at college?'

'Yeh.'

'Hey yeh! What college you at?'

'Columbia.'

'I went upstate, to Purchase.'

'Yeh?'

Both young men were clean shaven, both wore blue jeans. One stood with his legs apart. He rocked on the side of his feet, calves tensed. The other had his weight on one leg and scuffed at the top step with his free foot.

'Can a couple of guys from Columbia spare a man from Purchase a dime?'

The student who had been scuffing with his foot fumbled in his jeans pocket for change. The other turned away to look out over Fifth Avenue.

Why was I in an iconoclastic mood? There was no doubt that New York had me in its thrall. Why resist? The city was big, it was famous, it was seamy, and so on. It was in the nature of a potent myth that it made us want to believe. There was the perception that anything might happen in that city. Everything which did happen to a visitor there became a 'New York Story', carried home like booty to be shown to friends and family.

I looked at my watch. It was nearly three o'clock.

My pattern of thought, that day, had begun as I rode the D-train. The D-train surfaced as it left Brooklyn and crossed the East river by the Manhattan Bridge. As the train came off the bridge I had noticed the long side wall of a nearby building. There were a couple of windows set arbitrarily in the huge expanse of sooty brick, and several others that had been bricked up over the years, the outline of the old lintels and sills still visible. An adjoining building had at some time been demolished from part of the lower half of the wall, leaving a clear scar. At the top left-hand side were the bleached remnants of a painted advertisement in green and white.

As the wall receded and the train re-entered its tunnel my thoughts coalesced. This was a perfect example of the irony of human perception. The wall, a tangible object, constructed years ago brick by brick was, at the same time, perfectly abstract. It was, certainly, a concrete realisation of the human imagination, a fabrication impossible in the natural world. But, more than that, the wall was a two-dimensional plane. The silhouette of the windows, the outline of the demolished building, the faded rectangle of the sign, the varied patina of the brickwork; these things all became a total composition of abstract form and colour. Of course New York had become the bastion of abstract painting in the 1940s. The whole city was an abstraction. What else was this colossal pile of ragged blocks and planes? The painters were steeped in their visual environment and had naturally reflected it in their art.

Then why had it taken so long for abstraction to be accepted as a form of reality? The buildings of Manhattan remained just that – a collection of specific buildings. And yet the idea of Manhattan was so much more than that! Myths, myths, myths, I muttered to myself.

'Are you receiving visitors?'

I looked up, startled. Elizabeth was standing in front of me. In the instant before I recognised her I saw Elizabeth as an unknown attractive young woman.

'Hi there,' she said.

'Sorry, I was thinking.'

'Is that what you were doing?' She was smiling at me. 'Sorry I'm late. There was a track fire and I had to wait an hour for the train to move.'

'Poor you. I'm fine, I've been people-watching.'

'You've caught Moishe's disease.'

I laughed. 'His enthusiasm anyway. Do you want to go inside and look at some art?'

'I'd prefer to go for coffee; my legs are aching and I'd kill to sit down.'

'Coffee? Yes, of course.'

'Don't worry, you can have hot chocolate if you like.'

I laughed again.

Elizabeth suddenly leant forward and kissed me lightly on the lips, then turned and began going down the steps. Before following her I looked behind me. The man in the greatcoat had been watching. He grinned at me and winked with both eyes in quick succession.

TWENTY-EIGHT
EMMA AND SASHA

My narrow bed now held two human bodies, closely pressed together. My room was no longer dark; a soft, soothing light seemed to come from somewhere. As in a dream I heard sweet, endearing words breathed in my ear, like the soft, beautiful Russian lullabies of my childhood. I became drowsy, my thoughts in confusion.

Lying in bed with Alexander Berkman for the first time, Emma Goldman began to think about the political meeting they had just left. Johann Most, a leader of the radical movement in New York, had called for acts of violent revenge for the execution of five anarchists in Chicago.

Most was an idealist, yet he, too, urged extermination. Could idealists be cruel? The enemies of life and joy and beauty are cruel. They are relentless, they have killed our great comrades. But must we, too, exterminate?

I was roused from my drowsiness as if by an electric current. I felt a trembling, shy hand tenderly glide over me. Hungrily I reached for it, for my lover. We were engulfed in a wild embrace. Again I felt terrific pain, like the cut of a sharp knife. But it was numbed by my passion, breaking through all that had been suppressed, unconscious, and dormant.

The morning still found me eagerly reaching out, hungrily seeking. My beloved lay at my side, asleep in blissful exhaustion. I sat up, my head resting on my hand. Long I watched the face of the boy who had so attracted and repelled me at the same time, who could be so hard and whose touch was yet so tender. Deep love for him welled up in my heart – a feeling of certainty that our lives were linked for all time. I pressed my lips to his thick hair and then I, too, fell asleep.

On November the eleventh, 1887, in Chicago, five men who had been found guilty of killing several policemen were hung. Another three served long jail terms. The ruthlessness of these sentences was a major stimulant to revolutionary activity in the United States. Emma Goldman was first attracted to radical politics at this time. The policemen were killed when a bomb went off while they were breaking up a meeting protesting against police brutality. It was never ascertained who threw the bomb but the press called for retribution against the speakers at the meeting.

. . . the trial proved the worst frame-up in the history of the United States. The jury was picked for conviction; the District Attorney announced in open court that it was not only the arrested men who were the accused, but that 'anarchy was on trial' and that it was to be exterminated. The judge repeatedly denounced the prisoners from the bench . . . The witnesses were terrorised or bribed . . .

Homestead was not an isolated event. The political atmosphere was continually recharged. In 1897, for instance, twenty-one strikers were shot by a sherriff and his posse at Hazleton, Pennsylvania. Shortly after Berkman was imprisoned, Goldman also spent a year in jail 'for urging revolution, violence and bloodshed'. She became a major if harassed figure in American political life, travelling on lecture tours, speaking at rallies, demanding change.

Well before Homestead, when Berkman and Goldman were new lovers, Berkman was already totally uncompromising in argument about the 'cause'.

> 'Artists are inspired people,' I said, 'everything comes easy to them.'
>
> 'Of course,' Berkman retorted, 'because the people work for them.'

In anger he might walk out of the house without a goodbye and remain away several days. After one such absence he asked permission to come to Goldman's room:

> . . . he began to talk, pouring out his whole soul. He said he loved me dearly . . .
>
> He told me about the famous Russian revolutionary catechism that demanded of the true revolutionist that he give up home, parents, sweetheart, children, everything dear to one's being. He agreed with it absolutely and he was determined to allow nothing to stand in the way. 'But I do love you,' he repeated. His intensity, his uncompromising fervour, irritated and yet drew me like a magnet. Sasha, my own wonderful, dedicated, obsessed Sasha, was calling. I felt entirely his.

Sasha is the diminutive for Alexander. Emma Goldman called her lover Sasha or, at times, Dushenka. Sasha told her little about himself, except that he had been expelled from school, in Russia, for writing an anti-religious essay and that he had left home for good.

Sometime after Sasha was imprisoned Goldman formed another relationship, with Ed Brady. Her new lover was far more sexually satisfying than Sasha had been but emotionally Berkman still held her.

. . . Sasha, our life together, his act, his martyrdom – every moment of the five years since I had first met him I now relived with poignant reality. Why was it, I mused, that Sasha was still so deeply rooted in my being? Was not my love for Ed more ecstatic, more enriching? Perhaps it was his act that had bound me to him with such powerful cords.

Through the years of Sasha's prison term, Goldman and his other friends made numerous attempts to have him released. At first his complete lack of faith in the American legal system caused Sasha to reject any appeal on his behalf. Later, when he agreed to his friends acting for him, the attempts were unsuccessful. It was not until May 1906, after serving fourteen of his twenty-two years, that Sasha was released.

Emma waited at the station for the train to arrive.

Someone was tugging at my sleeve, voices were calling: 'Emma! Emma! The train is in. Quick – to the gate!' . . . I remained riveted to the ground, clutching at the post, my heart throbbing violently.

My friends returned, a stranger walking between them, with swaying step . . . That strange looking man – was that Sasha, I wondered. His face deathly white, eyes covered with large, ungainly glasses; his hat too big for him, too deep over his head – he looked pathetic, forlorn. I felt his gaze upon me and saw his outstretched hand. I was seized with terror and pity . . . I put the roses I had brought into his hand, threw my arms around him, and pressed my lips to his. Words of love and longing burned in my brain and remained unsaid. I clung to his arm as we walked in silence.

At a restaurant the group of friends ordered food and wine.

We drank to Sasha. He sat with his hat on, silent, a haunted look in his eyes. Once or twice he smiled, a painful, joyless grin. I took off his hat. He shrank back embarrassed, looked about furtively, and silently put his hat on again. His head was shaved. Tears welled up into my eyes; they had added a last insult to the years of cruelty; they had shaved his head and dressed him in hideous clothes to make him smart at the gaping of the outside world. I choked back my tears and forced a merry tone, pressing his pale, transparent hand.

Eventually they were alone together.

We looked at each other like children left in the dark. We sat close, our hands clasped, and I talked of unessential things, unable to pour out what was overflowing in my heart. Utterly exhausted, I wearily dragged myself to bed. Sasha, shrinking into himself, lay down on the couch. The room was dark, only the gleam of Sasha's cigarette now and then piercing the blackness. I felt stifled and chilled at the same time. Then I heard Sasha groping about, come close, touch me with trembling hands.

We lay pressed together, yet separated by our thoughts, our hearts beating in the silence of the night. He tried to say something, checked himself, breathed heavily, and finally broke out in fierce sobs that he vainly tried to suppress. I left him alone, hoping that his tortured spirit might find relief in the storm that was shaking him to the roots. Gradually he grew calm and said he wanted to go out for a walk, the walls were crushing him. I heard him close the door, and I was alone in my grief.

Berkman recovered physically but was alienated from a world which had continued to change while he had been held in the past.

Everything in the present . . . made him wince and avoid it. It was a bitter irony that I, of all Sasha's friends, should cause him the deepest disappointment and pain – I who had never had him out of my mind in all the cruel years, or out of my heart, no matter who else had been there, not even Ed, whom I had loved more deeply and intensely than anyone else. Yet it was I who most roused Sasha's impatience and resentment; not in a personal sense, but because of the changes I had undergone in my attitude to life, to people, and to our movement. We did not seem to have a single thought in common. Yet I felt bound to Sasha, bound forever by the tears and blood of fourteen years.

TWENTY-NINE
THE THING

'What was Frick's wife like?'

We were having coffee at a place on Lexington Avenue. Elizabeth reached under the table and rubbed her legs as she spoke.

'What was she like? When I think of it I realise she's only mentioned a few times in the biography. I don't even know exactly how many children they had. I suppose Harvey thought it indelicate to discuss personal matters.'

'Is that Victorian reticence or was the author concentrating on Frick's business machinations?'

'Frick certainly was reticent.' I was briefly distracted by a passing waitress who had a huge brown birthmark on the back of her calf. I looked back to Elizabeth who was smiling and shaking her head.

'Moishe has definitely corrupted you.'

I laughed, somewhat nervously.

'Anyway, I was about to tell you something about Frick's reticence. Quite late in his career, as an eminent capitalist, Frick met with James Stillman at the National City Bank. A journalist they both respected approached them for their opinion on the bearish state of the stock market. After discussing the matter for an hour they released a statement: "The USA is a great and growing country. Signed James Stillman; Henry C. Frick. This is confidential and not for publication unless names are omitted." '

'Holy shit, imagine being married to the man, trying to talk to him. You'd think his wife would have sent Berkman a thankyou letter.'

'Perhaps he was more forthcoming in private.'

'A big perhaps.'

'Yes. In the public record, anyway, Frick's facade is like a flat plane of well-polished rock. There's little difference in the few angles I can approach it from and I slip off the surface at every attempt.'

'Isn't this thing starting to take on the proportions of an obsession?'

'I can use the defence that I was brought up to pursue things to their underlying cause, never to rely on the up-front publicity, the accepted truths. In this case I hoped Sasha Berkman would lead me somewhere. At first I imagined he only added symmetry to the expected pattern, the symmetry of contradiction. But the sense of tragedy, self-propelled tragedy, that surrounds his story has left me disquieted. And then I feel Harvey does reveal small glimpses of something possibly human in Frick.'

The waitress with the birthmark passed us again.

'While I risk boring you with my obsession, there's a story I'd like to tell you, this time about Sasha Berkman. He tried to escape from jail through a tunnel. Do you want to hear it?'

'Sure, but isn't this where Hollywood takes over from history?'

'I promise you, I invent nothing. Berkman actually devised a code and managed to smuggle messages out of the jail to some of his friends. They gathered a team and rented a house almost directly opposite the front gate of the prison. Berkman planned the tunnel to be dug from the cellar of the house. It would go beneath the gate and come up under an outhouse in the prison yard. Somehow he would make his way unobserved to the outhouse, pull up the floor boards and crawl through the tunnel to the house. But the actual digging turned out to be slow and expensive. The tunnellers hit rock near the prison wall and had to dig beneath the foundations. As they dug deeper they released poisonous fumes which caused yet further delay while a machine was installed to draw in fresh air. To save time and money the tunnel was kept very narrow and the men had to lie down on their stomachs and drill with one hand. As you can imagine, they could only work for half-hour shifts in such conditions. They arranged for a pianist to come to the house. She played while they worked to cover the sounds of the digging. At any sign of danger she stopped and pressed an electric button. Staccato piano chords signalled that work could recommence.'

'Is this for real?' Elizabeth was looking at me suspiciously.

'Why would I lie to you? Honestly, the story is recounted in Emma Goldman's autobiography. Anyway, they eventually completed the work. The team broke up and returned to New York, leaving one man, Tony, who alone knew the key to Sasha's code. Unfortunately, Tony turned out to have acted with quirkish independence. Instead of bringing the tunnel up in the outhouse he had re-routed it to the middle of the prison yard. Sasha became alarmed, but what could he do? When he tried to make his escape at the new point he found it covered with a pile of rocks. A new building was being put up in the yard and a wagon load of stone had been dumped, on the exact location of the tunnel. Sasha was now in a desperate state. He communicated with Tony who agreed to go to New York to re-assemble the team and raise more money to complete the tunnel as originally planned.

'While Tony was away some children found their way into the empty house and discovered the secret passage. One of their parents was not only the agent for the house but also a guard at the jail. So that was that.'

'Was anyone caught?' asked Elizabeth.

'The police and prison officials couldn't find any evidence about the excavation. They were astounded by the daring of the scheme and the quality of the engineering. The police claimed it had been meant for a prominent forger who was serving a long term. The prison authorities suspected Sasha and, although there was no evidence, put him in solitary confinement. He rotted there for over a year.'

As we finished our coffee we decided to walk across Central Park to the West Side and eat somewhere before catching the train home. The late afternoon sun lit the park eerily. While we were indoors there had been a brief thunderstorm. Water was still dripping from the trees. The tops of the apartment towers on Central Park West gleamed clearly against a backdrop of departing black clouds.

'The waitress with the birthmark reminded me of something.' Elizabeth looked half round at me as we walked. 'I know a woman who has two identical twin sisters called Connie and Sally. They are what is called "left and right" identicals. Have you heard of this before?'

'No, never.'

'One is left-handed, the other right-handed; one has a mole on her left breast, the other on her right breast, and so on.'

I looked at Elizabeth. She was smiling at me mischievously.

'Until recently Connie was married to a guy called Bryce. But now Bryce has left Connie and has moved in with Sally. No one in either of their families is speaking to the new couple. Sally says everything will be OK – people forget.'

'Is this a cautionary tale about the dangers of pursuing symmetry in one's life?'

'Maybe,' she said, laughing, 'but I was more interested in the way people adapt to change. Do you think Sally's family would eventually accept this situation?'

'Perhaps, but I find it hard to believe Connie would.'

'Yes.' Elizabeth sounded reflective.

We had come to a park bench. It was wet and studded with bird droppings. Elizabeth found some tissues in her handbag and wiped the seat for us to sit down.

'Are you getting homesick here?'

'No, not really. I don't have time to be.'

'Seriously, don't you miss your family and Australia?'

'I'd like to see my parents but I'm certainly not pining.'

'Moishe used to miss your family terribly. That was when he first came back, just before we were married.'

'I wonder what he missed. Moishe seems so totally of New York.'

'He missed the intimacy. He used to say he wanted us to make a family like yours. He was so impressed, so young then, almost a different human being.'

'I find it hard to imagine Moishe other than he is now.'

'The memory is shaky, even for me.'

'Anyway, he has paid my family back. I know I'll miss you as much.'

Elizabeth half smiled but her expression was preoccupied.

Moishe shouted out as we came in through the front door.

'Where have you people been! You're late for one of the classics of the 1950s.'

The house was in darkness so it must have been a television classic that we were missing. We entered the room and found Moishe with the two younger children clustered about him on the sofa.

'Where's Hannah?' asked Elizabeth.

'Homework,' said Moishe hurriedly and raised a forefinger to his lips. The commercial break was over. 'It's *The Thing*.'

I was about to ask him which 'thing' but thought better of speaking.

Elizabeth went upstairs. I stood for a minute considering whether I would go to my room and read. Instead I was drawn to the family group. On the television, small grey figures stood in a huddle engaged in some sort of heated debate. Without a purpose, without a plot these little people appeared faintly absurd. Within a few minutes of viewing they assumed character as part of a story. The 'Thing', I discovered, was an alien creature, a man-cum-plant, who was harassing an American scientific base amid northern ice and snow.

During the next break Moishe became voluble:

'These were the days when Hollywood gloried in storytelling. Even the cornball of the most popular movies was infused with a sense of drama. Look at this: you have the obsessed scientist who must communicate with the monster in the interests of pure knowledge, and you have the pragmatic soldier who must act to destroy a source of danger to human existence. In the outcome the practical man is proven right and wins the day, and everyone's faith in democracy, liberty and the American way is re-inforced. This was a society that still believed in itself. You missed the greatest scene. The Thing is frozen in a lump of ice and is being kept in the coolroom. The guard has wrapped himself in an electric blanket. OK, when the shift changes his replacement throws the blanket over the Thing because it is giving him the creeps. The camera pans to the plug of the electric blanket. Later we see water dripping from under the blanket as the block thaws. We're much too subtle for this nowadays. If someone made this movie now, it would be content-free and riddled with astounding special effects. We can't tell a story with a straight face anymore. So, all we have is technique.'

THIRTY
HOMESTEAD: THE VICTORY

Perhaps Henry Clay Frick's greatest talent was organisational. He quickly co-ordinated the various facets of his industry, mining, manufacture, transportation and sales, considering a scale far larger than he controlled. Partnership with Andrew Carnegie followed, Frick providing the coke for Carnegie's steel mills. In 1889 Frick became the shareholding chairman of the Carnegie Company. He set about studying the process of steel manufacture and thereby reorganised the management of the company, the largest steel maker in the world, incorporating the largest coke producer in the world and employing thirty thousand men.

George Harvey, describing the background to the strike at Homestead, wrote that Frick invited the union to negotiate in January 1892 and was ignored for two months. Frick considered the Homestead workforce of 3,800 men overpaid, and that some unskilled labourers were inequitably earning up to ten times more than their skilled counterparts. The company was heading for eventual bankruptcy. The union and Frick were natural adversaries waiting to test each other's power. The final differences in negotiations were not vital:

> . . . but for extrinsic considerations of prestige . . . So no further concession was offered by either side and the issue of dominance, if not of actual control, between capital and labor, personified by owners and unions, was squarely joined and Mr. Frick, relying upon

the inviolability of 'property', no less than 'life and liberty', guaranteed by the Constitution, decided to close the mills on July 1st and to reopen them, unless prevented by force, on July 6th.

When the Congressional inquiry into the Homestead confrontation asked Frick why he had used Pinkerton guards he replied:

Because we did not see how else we could get protection. We only wanted them for watchmen to protect our property and see that workmen we would take to Homestead – and we had had applications from many men to go there to work – were not interfered with.

We brought the watchmen here as quietly as possible; and had them taken to Homestead at an hour of the night when we hoped to have them enter our works without any interference and without meeting anybody. We proposed to land them on our own property, and all our efforts were to prevent the possibilities of a collision between our former workmen and our watchmen.

Rifle fire was opened on the barges carrying the Pinkertons within a mile of Homestead and continued until they passed the town and drew into the landing place on the firm's property. As the mob of over a thousand were clambering down the bank, Captain Heinde, in charge of the Pinkertons, was shot in the thigh while confronting a young worker on the landing stage. Instantly the crowd along the bank charged forward, pelting the barges with bullets. Firing for the first time the Pinkertons repelled the attack with only twelve rifles.

During the lull which followed, the Pinkertons attempted to decide on a course of action. With Captain Heinde unconscious no one was willing to take responsibility for unpacking the boxes of rifles in the hold. The tugboat retreated with the wounded, leaving the barges to manage as they could.

Surrounded by thousands of blood thirsty enemies bent soley upon their complete extinction and equipped with all diabolical agencies of destruction, they could not even fight for their lives. Anyone who showed a head for an instant at a hatchway or porthole gasping for a breath of air was pelted with bullets by sharpshooters; oil was pumped upon the surface of the water and set on fire; natural gas, directed from a large main, was exploded by rockets; dynamite was hurled upon the barges to blow them to bits; burning rafts were floated down to set them on fire; cannon blazed at them from the opposite bank; – such was the inferno in which the prisoners barely existed until, without hope of succor and destitute even of food, they raised a white flag in token of surrender, only to see it riddled by bullets.

The eventual surrender of the Pinkertons is described by a Mr Bridge who collected his information from newspaper accounts of the time.

For nearly a mile the watchmen walked, ran, or crawled through a lane of infuriated men, women, and children; and at every step they were struck with fists, clubs, and stones. Their hats, satchels and coats were snatched away from them; and in many cases they were robbed of their watches and money. Not a man escaped injury. One of them, Connors, unable to move and defend himself, was deliberately shot by one of the strikers and then clubbed. Another, named Edwards, also wounded and helpless, was clubbed by another striker with the butt end of a musket. Both of these men died; and another became insane and committed suicide as a result of the fearful beating received after surrender. About thirty others were afterwards taken to the hospital with broken arms and disjointed ankles, shattered noses, gouged eyes, bruised heads, and injured backs.

1892 was an election year. Neither the Republicans nor the Democrats wished to antagonise the votes of working-men throughout the country. Tariff protection of the steel industry might be reduced by either party if the union was dealt with too harshly. All the stockholders of the Carnegie Company were life-long members of the Republican party and Andrew Carnegie was himself a public supporter of unionism. 'Thou shalt not seek thy neighbour's job' was his adage.

But what of Frick? In his view the workers' action was organised rebellion. There had been no strike, no lockout. Work had simply ceased automatically when the time fixed for coming to a new employment agreement had expired. When Whitelaw Reid intervened privately, after the appeal from Hugh O'Donnell, requesting that the union be recognised in exchange for all demands being dropped, Frick's reaction was predictable. A representative visited Frick's sick bed, finding his face and head swathed in bandages.

> . . . Mr. Frick declared emphatically that he would never consent to settle the difficulties if President Harrison himself should personally request him to do so. Notwithstanding the fact that he was a Republican and a warm friend and admirer of the President, the whole Cabinet, the whole leadership of the party might demand it but he would not yield. He was going to fight the strike out on the lines that he had laid down. I remarked 'If it takes all summer?' 'Yes,' he said, 'if it takes all summer and all winter, and all next summer and all next winter. Yes, even my life itself. I will fight this thing to the bitter end. I will never recognise the Union, never, never!'

In the court battle which followed, Chief Justice Paxton declared that:

> It was not a cry of 'bread or blood' from famished lips or an ebullition of angry passions from a sudden outrage or provocation. It was a deliberate attempt of men without a grievance to wrest from others their lawfully acquired property and to control them in their use and enjoyment of it.
>
> A mere mob, collected upon the impulse of the moment, without

any definite object beyond the gratification of its sudden passions, does not commit treason, although it destroys property and takes human life. But when a large number of men arm and organise themselves by divisions and companies, appoint officers, and engage in a common purpose to defy the law, to resist its officers, and to deprive any portion of their fellow citizens of the rights to which they are entitled under the Constitution and laws of the Commonwealth of Pennsylvania, it is levying of war against the State, and the offence is treason.

In November, Republican President Harrison was defeated in a landslide by the Democrat candidate, Cleveland. Frick, acting for the company, had contributed twenty-five thousand dollars to the Republican campaign. Frick wrote to Carnegie: 'I am very sorry for President Harrison but I cannot see that our interests are going to be affected one way or the other by the change in administration.' Carnegie replied, 'I fear that Homestead did much to elect Cleveland – very sorry – but no use getting scared.'

Frick, writing to his partner on the twenty-first of November, was finally jubilant:

Strike officially declared off yesterday. Our victory is now complete and most gratifying. Do not think we will ever have any serious labor trouble again . . . Let the Amalgamated still exist and hold full sway at other people's mills. That is no concern of ours.

THIRTY-ONE
WARBURGS 3

Water cascaded down the Volkswagen windscreen. Revolving brushes scuffed at the side windows through jets of spray. I sat beside Moishe in the front seat, sharing in a ritual which was totally new to me.

'Do you ever think about the word *wife*? Wife,' Moishe repeated the word solemnly. 'It sounds like old English, Anglo-Saxon. There are other words, words like *bread* and *womb*. These words instil confidence, and feelings of well being.'

The car edged forward, the wheels on the driver's side drawn on a slow moving track. The jets hit the car in torrents, and large brushes, hardly visible through the streaming water, spun and bounced about us like a volley of beach balls.

'This is one of the few first-hand sensual experiences left us in this century. Most things else are vicarious. I come to the car wash whenever I need contact with the physical world, whenever I need solace. Here I think of words like *bread* and *wife* and *womb*. In fact, this is my womb away from the womb.' Moishe laughed and leant forward so that his head was almost touching the windscreen. Light through the rushing water played in patterns on his face.

We had just come from Warburgs completing two errands: the weekly shopping, and our long-standing agreement to watch people in their summer clothes passing through the carpark. That day Warburgs stank. The smell hit me as soon as I pushed our trolley in through the automatic sliding doors. Moishe left me to select the dairy products while he began the main body of our shopping. My progress down the aisle was slow. Someone had dropped a large tub of plain yogurt. The thick white tracery of yogurt on the linoleum remained as a record of the velocity of the tub's impact with the floor. I was still distracted by the smell of the supermarket. It was not a simple smell. Whatever its basis, it was overlaid and masked by other odours: by the smell of freshly baked bread, of soap and disinfectant, of vegetables and fruit. My nose was unable to separate enough of these odours to distinguish what lay beneath them. I took two large cardboard containers of whole milk, which would be used chiefly to satisfy Herman's constant need for breakfast cereal at all times of the day and night.

At the cash register we were held up by a woman arguing with the checkout girl about the value of her coupons. Moishe had pride in his ability to choose the fastest-moving checkout line. He felt this woman cast an unreasonable slur on his judgement. Around us other queues moved rapidly while the woman, a short person wearing a gold hair net, made her scene. Moishe suddenly stepped forward and pushed his wallet under the woman's nose.

'How much do you want?'

'What are you talkin' about?'

'Look lady, you may come here to play with bits of coloured paper but the rest of us want to do our shopping. We like to do it quick and get out of the place.' He took out a ten dollar note from his wallet and waved it in front of her. She snatched the note, threw her coupons on the counter and walked out of the supermarket leaving her groceries behind, piled up at the cash register.

Despite the heat Lake Warburgs was half-full. There had been a brief thunderstorm late the previous afternoon. Moishe drew the car out into the water a little, to give us an unobstructed view of the entrance of the supermarket. He turned off the engine and wound down his window.

'Let us see what comes to pass,' he said. In front of us heat rose off the asphalt, mildly distorting the posters advertising Specials, which were stuck to the facade of the building. 'Leg of Lamb: $2.99 lb.' seemed to shimmer on the wall. I blinked several times as though trying to focus a picture blurred through a camera viewfinder. Shoppers, also gently shimmering, were coming and going through the supermarket doors.

'Sex so thoroughly informs our view of humanity,' said Moishe. 'When I look at the men among these people I'm bored. If I try to see them through women's eyes I find them ridiculous. But the women are all interesting to look at. Whether they are young or old, pretty or plain, they have potential or at least history. Every woman is part of a vast biological system, a sexual map of the species. Of course, this is true of the men too, but for me, a heterosexual male, they are all phantoms physically. This is what my eyes tell me.'

'What does your brain tell you?' I felt an urge to tease Moishe.

'Oh, let's leave my brain out of it, or things will get complicated. We're here to watch people, so why not be real voyeurs.'

We looked ahead through the windscreen, in silence, for several minutes.

'Well, what do you see?'

'What do I see?' I said. 'I feel as though I'm sitting for an Art History slide test, with people instead of paintings projected for me to identify and compare.'

'You're not getting into the right spirit, kid. Summon your hormones, become sensually aroused and lascivious. Remember our discussion here in the winter and have a real good look at these bodies transformed in their summer clothes.'

I looked at the passersby again. I understood Moishe, but felt reality did not always conform with his requirements. From Warburgs came middle-aged and elderly couples, and mothers with young children riding on their shopping carts. From the Carvel ice-cream store next to the supermarket came a group of teenagers in swimming suits and loose tee-shirts. The clothes these people wore were now spare. There were some bare feet, tanned arms and legs. There was a powerful sense of human presence; a pattern of raised voices interwoven with popular music from car radios.

'Do you know something?' Moishe looked round from our moving view through the windscreen. 'History may never recognise this, but both your parents, your mother and your father, are great men.'

'My mother might argue the point.'

'Well, they are both great women too.' He turned back to the window. 'Just a minute, I'm going to contradict myself. How old do you think *he* is?' Moishe pointed out a man who was walking towards us.

'Late twenties, early thirties.'

'Yes, I'd say early thirties. Look at the son of a bitch. It's well over eighty degrees. The humidity is fantastically high and he's wearing a suit and tie. Have you ever considered the incredible resilience of the business suit as a social institution? In the sixties a generation rejected the suit as a symbol of a repressive social order. This man who's passing us – look, you can see the sweat on his face – he would have grown up in that era of hard rock and rebellion. I've always looked with interest at that generation. You see, I just missed it, sneaking in at the end of the jazz age, a bebop cat with smatterings of soul and early rock-and-roll. Had I been born a few years later I'd probably be made in a different mould. I'd probably be talking to you about different things. I might be a jaded idealist, a former junkie, I might even play guitar. Anyway, the point of all this is that the suit survived and is still doing very well.'

As Moishe spoke a cloud briefly covered the sun, transforming the scene outside our window. The passing figures turned flat and colourless and then, as suddenly, popped out again in full relief as the cloud departed.

'Now there's this period my own kids are growing up in. It has no music at all that I'm willing to recognise as such. I think of Hannah and the past she will have to claim, a past of background noise.'

'She'll probably see it differently.'

'Maybe. Now look at this piece.' Moishe pointed out a young woman who was getting out of a car nearby. Totally unprompted, the phrase *the lineaments of desire* occurred to me.

'Biologically speaking,' said Moishe, 'this kid is hot property.'

Moishe went on talking, analysing the young woman as she walked towards the supermarket. But, I was no longer concentrating on what he had to say. I watched the woman, absorbed in my own perception of her movements. At that moment, it seemed that no one, particularly not Moishe, could understand what I was seeing.

The Volkswagen rolled slowly forward. Long strips of heavy felt-like material were draped around us, sliding across the car as it moved.

'What do you think of the word *wife*?'

'As a sound or as someone to love and cherish?'

'Both, the whole glorious picture.'

'It's hardly something that has been central in my life.'

'But you should take the wider, social view. Look at the wonderful institution of marriage, the channelling of concupiscence into a single, exclusive relationship. The divorce rate may climb but people still long to take a husband or wife. It's a matter of romance, of nest building and cosiness. "I just want to be loved by you, by you and nobody else but you." ' As Moishe sang to me the car eased forward through a massive blast of hot air. The water on the windscreen flattened and scattered from the glass and finally we rolled back out into daylight.

THIRTY-TWO
COLLECTOR

In 1901, at the age of fifty-two, Frick retired as a business executive. He was now a capitalist of the first rank, his personal fortune estimated at some fifty million dollars. During the previous decade he had overseen an eightfold increase in the Carnegie Company's earnings. He had gone through a long and tortuous rift with Carnegie himself, who had sought to force him from his position and shareholding on unfavourable terms. In the end Frick won the contest.

In his retirement Frick's time was divided between three approximately equal interests: investment, recreation and art. His major area of investment was in the United States railway system. 'Railroads,' he declared, 'are the Rembrandts of investment.' As usual he was methodical, thoroughly acquainting himself with the business practices of particular railway companies, down to the details of bookkeeping, before taking out a financial interest in them. True to his own beginnings he was attracted to enterprises willing to risk judicious extravagance rather than false economy. But he never speculated by trading on margins nor attempted to break up a company rather than contribute to its development. He became the largest individual railway stockholder in the world.

The third of Frick's time spent in recreation was less focused. He toyed with building a yacht of his own design but abandoned the project before beginning construction. The idea of golf he found slow and tedious until, after following a group of friends round the course after luncheon at a club, he tried the game and was immediately hooked. 'Golf in the morning' was frequently recorded in his diary as many as six times a week. Bridge often filled the afternoon, or when there were no partners available he was content playing solitaire by the hour. He loved to give small luncheons, with attractive women included:

. . . and large dinners to 'interesting' men rather than exclusively to business associates. An admirable host, he attended to every detail, arranging the placing of guests and personally distributing their cards to avert possibilities of error.

Then there was art. But, before looking at the collector, what more did George Harvey tell me about Frick's character?

The physical attractiveness of his boyhood ripened into a highly distinguished appearance in his later years, never failing, greatly to his annoyance, to draw the attention of onlookers when he passed along a street or through a railway station. Not that he was shy; he was fully composed under all conditions; he was simply, innately, modest. But his squarely moulded head and finely chiseled features, illumed by a pair of twinkling, though scrutinizing eyes, combined to make of him a notably handsome man. And he always dressed the part, usually in dark blue cloth with a hairline stripe and without a suspicion of jewellry showing.

His voice was low, soft and melodious and was never raised. Whatever annoyance or resentment he ever felt appeared in the expression of those eyes, which could become 'very steely' very quickly. Invariably courteous to a degree, his minor manners were, as the discerning and somewhat critical Professor Sage of Harvard remarked once upon a time, 'literally exquisite, without a trace of affectation' . . .

Paradoxically, his notably quick mind did not respond readily to wit; he hardly ever laughed . . .

Asked . . . what was the secret of his success, he replied sententiously:

'Work and sleep. My alarm clock is always set eight hours ahead of the time I go to bed and I have trained both body and mind to relax. But hard work is the thing. During the first six years with the Steel company I reached my office every weekday morning between seven and eight and never left till six. I walked enough to keep fit and became actually robust. In fact, if I hadn't been pretty husky when assaulted I probably shouldn't have got off as well as I did. Carnegie often remarked to me, "You certainly do get work out of those fellows". I did, too. It was the force of example. When they saw what their Chairman was doing they all followed suit gladly and enthusiastically. So we got on very well.'

While he was still a teenager the walls of Frick's rooms were covered with whatever prints and drawings he could find in his remote setting and with his small income. The explanation Harvey gives for the origin of this interest is that it was unquestionably innate. In 1881, after securing his first million, the future founder of the Frick Collection travelled to Europe with Andrew Mellon, the future founder of the National Gallery. While on this trip Frick bought his first European painting, a narrative piece by Luis Jiminez called *In the Louvre*. It was not until 1895 that he began to buy paintings in large numbers. In that year he bought fifteen works, largely by French artists now considered minor.

Frick approached collecting with the thorough study and organisation familiar in his business practice. He continually resold paintings following a relentless pursuit of the best works obtainable. Not one of the first thirty-five paintings he bought remains in the final collection, and it was after the turn of the century, with his concentrated activity in retirement, that the focus of his buying became clear.

A visit to the Wallace Collection in London inspired Frick to make his own as complete and perfect as possible for ultimate exhibition. The site of the former Lennox Library at Seventieth Street and Fifth Avenue was bought and his 'palace' built at the cost of $5,400,000. In 1914 the Frick family moved in, and Mrs Frick continued to live there after her husband's death. The building was converted and extended on her death and opened to the public in 1935. The final collection had cost between thirty and forty million dollars.

But what was Frick's attitude to the art he collected? What understanding underlay his choice of a body of work that has little historical or stylistic continuity but is united by consistent quality? Harvey gave me an enthusiastic gloss.

> Mr. Frick did not merely admire and enjoy beautiful pictures; he loved them with a passion as tender as he felt for little children. They rested him, refreshed his mind, soothed his spirit. Often late at night, at the end of a trying day, when perfect stillness reigned, he would slip noiselessly, almost furtivily, into the darkened gallery, turn on the lights and sit for an hour or more, first on one divan then on another, absorbing solace and happiness through the mirrors of his heart before seeking the mental and physical relaxation of dreamless sleep. And nothing gave him so much pleasure as quietly witnessing, himself unseen, the delights of enraptured visitors, and listening to their comments.

It seemed to me that Frick was not merely attracted to superficial qualities in painting. Unlike many American millionaires, his collection is not unduly represented by, for instance, paintings of handsome women and children or courtly portraits. There are the Fragonards and the Bouchers but his five favourite pictures are all truly extraordinary paintings: Bellini's *St. Francis*, Holbein's *Sir Thomas More*, Velasquez's *Phillip the Fourth*, Vermeer's *Lady with a Letter*, and, of course, the Rembrandt *Self-Portrait*.

Shortly before he died Frick remarked, 'I can only hope that the public will get one-half the pleasure that has been afforded me in enjoyment of these masterpieces in proper surroundings. I want this collection to be my monument.'

In October 1919 another child called Henry Clay Frick the second was born, Frick's fourth grandchild but first grandson. Early in November Frick became ill and was sent to bed, where he stayed for almost two weeks. After getting up he became impatient to visit his grandson, ignored the protests of his wife and daughter, and made the drive of over an hour. Complete exhaustion followed his return. His doctor refused to continue to attend a patient who had disobeyed his orders to stay in bed. Another physician was called but was unable to gain Frick's confidence. He died on the second of December. In his will Frick left five-sixths of his estate in public benefactions and bequests.

In a tribute to Frick's collection published simultaneously with the will, a Mr Cortissor wrote:

It is an interesting coincidence that, at the time when the historic interiors of Europe and Great Britain are being broken up as never before, the announcement of the Frick bequest should be made. The old order changeth, giving place to the new. Is the ancient tradition to be revived in the United States, ancestral collections being scattered abroad only to enter upon a more permanent form of existence on this side of the Atlantic?

THIRTY-THREE
COFFEE

Elizabeth sat on the edge of my bed, crying. I looked at her in dismay. Seconds before she had been lying beside me, her hands moving along my side. Suddenly she had turned away, slipped her legs over the edge of the bed and, sitting up, had begun to sob.

'What's the matter?' I reached up and touched her arm. She continued to cry steadily, without drama.

'Have I done something to hurt you?' Despite my concern I was fascinated by the change this emotion had caused in Elizabeth's face. Her usually compact identity had dissolved into a state of disarming childlike vulnerability.

'No, it's not that.'

'Is it Moishe?'

'No.' Her voice showed a trace of annoyance. She stopped crying and looked at me. 'You're so young.'

'What do you mean?' My response was reflexive. Without understanding what she meant I was already hurt.

'I was crying because you seem so young and so fragile.'

I stared at her.

'Don't be offended.' She quickly slid back into bed beside me and clasped my head in her hands. In the house it was quiet. There was no jazz in the living-room, no drums came from upstairs, no voices from the kitchen. Moishe was at a conference in Cleveland and the children were asleep in their rooms. Even the furnace was quiet, failing to punctuate the warm night with its sudden spasms of ignition. I lay still, trying to comprehend what Elizabeth was telling me. My senses were incredibly heightened, my heart was thumping distractingly, and I felt as though I would start crying involuntarily at any moment. Everything that happened in that household seemed calculated to astound me.

Earlier that night Elizabeth and I had sex five times. I am not sure how it began. I know that throughout the afternoon she plied me with coffee while we chatted in the kitchen. This is not an excuse. My disorientation was at the core of this experience but not an explanation for it. Even as we undressed, dropping clothes across the floor of my room, I felt the absurdity of the situation; our idiosyncratic bodies struggling free from their mass-produced clothing. As Elizabeth reached for me, still wearing her socks, I was afraid. I was looking at a woman who was completely unknown to me. Undressed she was middle-aged. She seemed short and heavy, and her body worn. I thought of Moishe.

Laughing, Elizabeth pushed me onto the bed and, after turning off my bedside light, came toppling down onto me. She wriggled forward, her thighs slipping over my hips luxuriously, and pushed a breast into my face. Under this assault my senses immediately responded. As we rolled over she reached down and, catching my penis in a tight fist, guided me into her.

'Push, come on, push!' she demanded. She grasped at my buttocks and drew me in forcefully.

'What about you?' I asked as she continued to pull me to her relentlessly.

'Fuck me, just fuck me!'

My disquiet grew as we screwed this way four times in succession. My mind wandered. I pictured sex scenes in movies. In Andy Warhol's *Heat* a young actor on the make couples with an aging actress on the stairs of her Hollywood house, his buttocks pumping with the short, hard movements and mechanical precision of two linked pistons. In Bertolucci's *Last Tango in Paris* Marlon Brando, standing up in his clothes, screws a woman whose name he does not even know. I scrambled through a vast panorama of vicarious love making, the bizarre public manifestations of ultimately private passions. And it seemed that these scenes were a part of my experience, were as real as what was happening to my body at that moment.

After my fourth orgasm Elizabeth got up and went to the lavatory. I lay in bed overheated, my skin prickling, my mind racing. What was going on here? I felt a wave of increasing dismay. It was as though my mind and my body had slipped into an irreconcilable double image, a sickening loss of myself from myself.

When I heard the quiet padding of Elizabeth's feet I looked around to see her body approaching as a black silhouette against the light from the next room. As she came closer the silhouette became solid, light rounding her body at its edges. I felt a small spark of recognition, that this woman was actually physically palpable, that I could reach out and touch her.

'How are you feeling?' she asked.

'Pretty strange.'

She knelt down beside the bed. I could see the moist luminosity of her eyes and the faint suggestion of her smile. And suddenly it seemed to me she was now returned to herself, was once again the person I knew. I leant forward and kissed her lips. For a few moments she remained crouched by the bed. I listened to her breathing. Then she slipped into bed beside me. As we lay on our sides looking at each other in the faint light I felt my own dislocation ease, my own body return to me. I brushed a hand across her nipples, over her stomach and down amongst the delicate wire of her pubic hair. The skin of her inner thighs was excruciatingly soft, half matter and half imagination, I thought. Slowly she lifted her free leg and gently placed it across my hip. This simple movement was, I knew, an act of trust.

'Please, don't be hurt,' Elizabeth said this as she moved her fingers through my beard. 'As you grow older youth seems increasingly fragile. That's all I meant.'

'You were crying because of this?'

'You can't know my youth.'

'Isn't youth a cheap commodity?'

Elizabeth was silent.

'Why cry for something you can't give me?'

She remained silent.

'Elizabeth, when we came to bed, why were you so aggressive?'

'I was angry,' she said, almost as a whisper.

'With me?'

'No, it had nothing to do with you. I was angry with Moishe.'

'Why?'

'I don't know.'

PART **TWO**

ONE

The narrow strip of land on which Island City was built was, in fact, a large sand bar. The whole suburban infrastructure was built on sand. Wooden power poles were set in massive concrete bases to eliminate movement. Top soil was trucked in for the gardens, a thin sustaining layer on top of sand and brine. The buildings had shallow basements in an attempt to remain above the water-table. The roads were fundamentally unstable and had to be patched constantly. Even so, I often heard cars scraping on the bitumen as they bounced and careered at high speed past me while I was out walking.

The long east-west running streets, which divided the four narrow blocks of houses, had generic names: Bayside Drive, Central Avenue and Beachview Boulevard. Similarly the short north-south running streets were simply numbered. The Feinbaums lived on 137th Street. The streets were all basically identical but for one consistent variant: the lower the street number the poorer the area became. 109th Street had flop houses, a halfway house for mental patients, a series of bars and cheap hostels, and Warburgs. From 148th Street for several blocks there was a golf course, its margins lined with large houses. They were wooden buildings, often white with green shutters on the windows, and usually having deep front verandahs. On the beach side there were brick apartment houses becoming taller and shabbier towards 109th Street.

My neighbour was practising the saxophone. It was an alto sax. He had been repeating the tune 'April in Paris' for over half an hour. Although my door was shut, and my neighbour's door was shut, the sound of his horn travelled insistently across the narrow landing. Our rooms were on the third floor of 187B 115th Street, a four-storey building owned by Milton and Myra Fishbach. 187B was on the beach block and from my room I could glimpse the Atlantic between apartment houses. My neighbour, whose name was Dwight Rubour, regularly practised his horn playing. He had a repertoire of 1930s standards: 'Star Dust', 'When Smoke Gets in Your Eyes', 'I Can't Get Started', 'Solitude' and so on. With Moishe's training I could distinguish this much now. As I sat at my desk, which I had picked up at a junk store on 109th Street, my work was steeped in this suburban echo of America's jazz heritage. On the street, particularly in Brooklyn, I was constantly passed by black kids who carried massive portable radios blasting out disco or rap. In my room the 1980s receded.

I had met Dwight Rubour several times on the narrow stairs of our rooming house. We simply exchanged a nod rather than entering into the many-faceted complication of speech. I had also met him outside the bathroom, which was on our landing and which we shared. Such meetings were infrequent – I suspect he had developed the technique of listening at his door for the sound of running water. He waited until I closed the bathroom door, and my door, before stepping out to take his turn. Either this was the case or there was an unusually consistent pattern to his chance movements. Sharing a bathroom with Dwight Rubour I noticed a number of details about him. He used a variety of multi-coloured, striped toothpaste which came in a clear tube. Once he left a book on the side of the bath. The title, *The Rape of Eden*, ran diagonally across the top half of the cover in bright yellow lettering above the photograph of a blonde woman wearing a low-cut red dress and holding a man's severed head in her hands. I knew that Dwight suffered from considerable hair loss, a fact borne out by the visibility of his scalp but fundamentally corroborated by deposits of hair regularly blocking the drain grill of the shower stall.

Living at 187B 115th Street was clearly different from the Feinbaums'. My room was very small. There was a narrow gap between my bed on one side of the room and my desk and the refrigerator on the other. At the end wall under the window was a little gas cooker and a sink. Elizabeth assisted me, occasionally, in my attempts to master the basics of food preparation. She had also lent me a rug for beside the bed and a kerosene lamp. We used the lamp for lighting more subtle than the long, flickering fluorescent tube on the ceiling. There was a narrow wardrobe but no chest of drawers, so most of my clothes stayed in the suitcase under the bed. It was early winter and the radiator under my desk constantly bumped and hissed with heat rising from the basement furnace. I had been in New York for nearly a year and at the Fishbachs' for four months.

As soon as Moishe returned from Cleveland I told him it was time I found an apartment. He was offended. Did I feel uncomfortable in his house? Of course not, but I thought his family had a right to some privacy. This, he said, was nonsense; I must stay. I told him I needed more quiet to get on with my study. This too was nonsense; I worked too hard as it was. Ruth and Herman begged me to stay. Only Hannah remained aloof.

This initial discussion, then, was inconclusive. But I began looking immediately for a suitable room to rent. My search led me towards 109th Street where the rents were low. Some of the rooms I looked at were virtually uninhabitable. Possibly the most extreme, on the fourth storey of a generally neglected building, had a hole in the wall where a door had once opened onto a balcony which no longer existed. There was a strip of sacking over the opening. The plaster was swollen and crumbling from the walls and ceiling. There was no sink, no cooker, no refrigerator and no bed.

The Fishbachs' room was better than most and, at twenty-five dollars a week, among the cheapest. There was no lease, the rent was payable monthly and the place basically clean. But my interview with Milton Fishbach was unusual.

'What do you think of Casper Weinberg?' These were his first words after I had explained why I was at his door. I looked at Mr Fishbach wondering what to say. He waited for my reply, legs astride, arms folded over his chest. He was, I guessed, in his seventies.

'I'm afraid I don't think much of the Reagan administration.'

He clasped my arm.

'I'll show you the room.'

As we came back downstairs he asked me if I were Irish.

'I'm from Australia.'

'That doesn't stop you being Irish.'

'That's true.' I smiled at Mr Fishbach.

'It's no joking matter boy, I won't have the fuckin' Irish in my house. OK, here's your key.'

'I won't be moving in for week or two.'

'That's fine, suit yourself, as long as you pay the rent.'

Milton Fishbach was, I discovered, an ardent Zionist. He had assumed that I disapproved of the United States administration because it was too liberal. Any other view was impossible. Over the following year I did not disillusion him. Steven Redman and I once filled a whole evening discussing this evasion of the truth. Were such tiny lies of omission unimportant? Could a case be made that meeting such minor, everyday confrontations with a sidestep was the root of social inertia? Was cowardice on a minute level actually worse than on a grand scale? In fact Mr Fishbach did not want to hear my opinion on any matter. But he loved to talk to me. Many times he stopped me on the garden path or in the entrance hall. I heard of the British attempt to doublecross the infant Jewish nation after the Second World War. I heard of

Tammany Hall and Irish police corruption in New York. I heard that Roosevelt and the New Deal were the beginning of the collapse of American society. I heard of New York in the thirties, when a meal at a diner cost twenty cents. This was New York before all the blacks moved up from the south and sent the city down the drain. Now everything of value was lost, all was morally decadent, gutless, cheap. Everyone was a mother fucker, a bastard, a son of a bitch, a cock sucker. Milton Fishbach was nasty and bitter, but he held his attitudes with energy, with insolent relish, and expressed them with obvious pleasure.

It took some time for me to tell Moishe I was leaving. I had been renting the room for two weeks, had bought the desk and made a trip to Warburgs for basic supplies. Uncharacteristically, he no longer protested, merely offering to help me move. It only took one trip in the larger car. Moishe carried my suitcase up the narrow stairs while I brought all my books and papers. This, I realise, was the only visit Moishe ever made to my apartment.

Elizabeth visited me every couple of days early in the morning, still warm from her shower, her hair smelling of shampoo, her body of soap.

My life seemed to have shifted into a completely new phase. At times I sat at my desk prepared for work but instead was distracted by the thought of my own behaviour. I was acting in a way which was alien to my experience but which I didn't want even to consider changing. I was enjoying myself, was enjoying Elizabeth thoroughly. But I could not avoid considering what this meant. Thoughts of Moishe hovered in my mind. Complicated ideas were habitual to me. I had grown up with thought as a fundamental discipline. I had been taught to observe, to discriminate, to search out underlying motivations. Admittedly I didn't see reality and morality in terms of strict black and white. I was aware of a great mass of grey, of the dilemmas, the contradictions that seemed to be intrinsically human. But now I was closely, quite possibly destructively, entwined in the lives of several other people. I felt I had to attempt to understand my own actions.

Then something happened which was totally unforseen. Three weeks after I left the Feinbaums' house Moishe moved out too. Elizabeth arrived at my door at ten-thirty at night in an extraordinary state. Moishe had confronted her that evening.

'He knows?'

Elizabeth laughed wildly, shaking her head. Her hands were pressed against my chest and I could feel her body heaving. I waited, bewildered.

'No, he says he loves me, but he can't stand my housekeeping any longer.'

'What?'

'He has already rented an apartment in Brooklyn, near the college.' She started laughing, or sobbing, again.

'Elizabeth! What is going on?'

'Tonight Moishe told me that he had no clean underwear in his drawer this morning.' She was completely calm for a moment. 'This apparently was the final straw. I can't keep my side of our partnership so he has had enough.'

'You have to be joking.'

'It's true.'

Suddenly she burst into hysterical tears and clung to me. As she cried I held her, looking over her shoulder at the bare wall. There was an undefined emotional void opening out within me. I felt as though I had been cheated of some basic premise on which I had relied heavily.

TWO

Steven Redman leant back on his chair so that it balanced on the two back legs. His shoulders rested against the dining-room wall, his bare legs were stretched on the table. I ran the index finger of my left hand around the rim of my wine glass.

It was a warm autumn evening. I had walked from my new apartment along the beach to visit Steven. Natalie was working late, as she usually did a couple of nights a week. I found Steven lying on the beach directly in front of his house reading a book. We sat on the sand for the last minutes of twilight watching people out strolling. No one was swimming. The water's edge was littered with unusual flotsam, a wide variety of medical packaging and waste, including syringes and dissected rats. A couple of children with jeans rolled halfway up their legs splashed in the gentle surf, hopping between plastic bundles and boxes which were washing back and forth. Steven made a mildly sarcastic comment about New York's waste disposal control. Mosquitoes, coming out with dusk, made us decide to move inside.

My glass began to vibrate with a high-pitched note under my moving finger.

'Is that a request for a refill?' Steve lowered his legs and reached forward to pour me burgundy from a glass flagon. 'How are you finding the experience of Island City tenancy?'

'It's fine but I've nothing much to compare it with. I lived at home in Australia.'

'You led a sheltered existence, it seems.'

'So I'm discovering.'

There was a pause while we looked at each other. How much did Steven know or understand?

'What the hell does Moishe think he's doing? Sometimes I can't figure the guy out.' Steve waved a hand in the air.

'I'm quite simply dumbfounded myself.'

We remained looking at each other for a few moments. Then Steven grunted and settled back against the wall again.

'Steve, I've been waiting for a chance to ask you about your politics.'

'I guess tonight's the night.'

'Do you mind?'

'No, not at all.'

'I've got the impression that you and Natalie differ –'

'Natalie considers herself a liberal humanist,' Steven interrupted me with the good-humoured impatience I had noticed in him before. He was usually keen to push a conversation forward, as though it might imminently uncover something of value. 'For me there's probably no such thing. There are capitalists and there are socialists, that's all that's likely.'

'And you are a socialist?'

'I'd like to say I'm a doctrinaire Marxist, if only to avoid admitting that I don't believe in anything. I'd hate to be considered a cynic.' Steven paused and grinned at me broadly. 'Look, I'll be dogmatic,' he contiued. 'If the word *capitalism* describes an economic and political system that's existed in the world for a number of centuries, then the word *socialism*, or *communism*, signifies the major contrary political force over the last century. Even though we choose to ignore it, Marxism has been *the* philosophy of this period. This has nothing to do with the relative merits of the two systems, it is merely a matter of fact. OK, if we go a stage further, Marx deduced that the overthrow of capitalism was intrinsic to its character and would take place as an inevitable historical process. My problem is that I can't believe in inevitability. I don't think that there's evidence that anything much *must* happen. That's where my dogma runs dry.'

'So, the words define the way the world is or could be. But what of the values the words stand for? Why can't Natalie be a liberal humanist.'

'She can probably be a potato if she wants it enough. In a capitalist society liberal humanism is the excuse people who've some sort of conscience use to make them feel better about being in positions of relative privilege. It's the comfortable middle-class, and not the people who are starving, who call themselves liberal humanists. But you see, I'm getting excited. I can't remain detached.'

'Why should you?'

'Because I'm sick of the stock answers, and I'm sick of the debate.'

'But, isn't there some interest left in speculation?'

'That's a nice way to put it. I guess I still like to speculate.'

'Speculation is a basic tenet for my family. I was brought up in a left-wing household. My parents implicitly believe in striving for evolutionary social change.'

'Sure, it's another idea. But nowadays the capitalists don't even apologise for capitalism's shortcomings. You know, the new materialism: let's celebrate our way to prosperity, let's do, let's believe, let's earn, let's save, let's consume and so on. It's a comfortable, self-congratulatory solution for those on top, and those with enough push to claw their way there.'

We sat in silence briefly. Steven began to rock on his chair.

'What capitalists fear is violent revolution,' he said. 'That's about all they do fear; their system is so wonderfully self-perpetuating.'

'Do you approve of violent change?'

'It doesn't matter what I approve of; I'm simply posing a view of reality. Moishe was probably right about *Dr. Strangelove*; nothing changes.'

'Why did you argue the opposite case with him?'

'I guess I get excited at times. Moishe's infernal calm makes me wild.'

'So you dismiss social activism and education?'

'And pluralism and tolerance? Oh sure, they're fine ideals but they allow the underprivileged to go on being screwed. You see, we also tolerate the right to exploit.'

'You have a pretty bleak view of the world.'

'It's a bleak world.'

'And you find it bleak.' I smiled at Steve and he joined me.

'Maybe I have a jaundiced outlook. Maybe I should look in my own mind for the problems. That would be a neat way to dismiss my pessimism. Maybe I get some sort of sick pleasure out of seeing everything black.'

'Alright Steve, I take the point. At least this way you're unlikely to have nasty surprises.' I paused, looking at him. Although large, Steven's body was thin and peculiarly angular. His elbows were out of proportion with his arms and enlarged at the joints as though by inflammation. What I had originally thought unnerving about him I now understood was a real ardour for any sort of vital contact. Cynicism was a protection. 'The other day,' I continued, 'I was doing some research; not Frick this time but my actual subject. I came across a piece about the cultural activities of the CIA.'

'The what?'

'That's what I thought. But apparently in the 1950s the CIA infiltrated legitimate cultural organisations in the States and Europe. As if that isn't enough, they were subtle about it. They didn't require these organisations to give blanket support to American policies because it was important to protect their apparent integrity and independence. In this way it was possible to attract eminent writers and intellectuals to unwittingly serve American interests.'

'But how, exactly?'

'Culture became a weapon in cold war propaganda. America was to be seen as the bastion of freedom and free expression. Abstract Expressionism became the perfect vehicle. It was American, it was new and vigorous and it was completely apolitical. The US Administration could embrace a school of painting which was only about painting. Where was the threat there? CIA money, largely channelled throught the Museum of Modern Art, sent this art abroad on exhibition.'

'And the artists were ignorant of it?'

'Probably, but how many artists try to control the use of their work if it is being widely and prestigiously exhibited? In any case, the movement was losing momentum as a creative force at the very point it was being taken up officially. Adolph Gottlieb predicted Abstract Expressionism would last a thousand years. It ruled for about ten. It suggests an unfortunate parallel with another Adolph and his thousand-year Reich.'

'I like it, I like the connection. You know, that whole time, the total insanity of McCarthyism, suggests to me a nation with a parochial identity, without the generosity of real confidence. We took on the role of world top dog and suddenly seemed to have everything to lose instead of everything to give. But what else could you expect from this system. The other day I was speculating about your Sasha Berkman. Imagine he'd shot and wounded a Rockefeller in 1950, what sentence do you think he'd have got?' Steven didn't give me time to answer. 'He'd have been framed with some larger conspiracy and put away for life, if not executed. And we believe in progress. Well, there may be a sort of progress after all, progress according to the dictates of the underlying social mores. You know, the object of your passion understood the political situation perfectly.'

I stared at Steve, perplexed.

'Don't look so scared. I'm talking about Frick. In his time the patterns were becoming entrenched. He understood the stakes. After all, what was Homestead if it wasn't a revolution?

Why else did they send in the National Guard? Homestead was revolution on a controllable scale. I'm sure Frick knew what was at issue.'

'I've wondered about that. But then again, it's hard to know how much his personality was reacting reflexively. In other words, how much are we pawns behaving according to our background?'

'Sure, we're pawns. Frick had a very clear world view which he didn't just invent. But he knew what he was up against and that he could land a permanent blow.'

'After the strike broke he wrote to Carnegie that he didn't care what happened elsewhere in the industry, *they* had won.'

'Well, perhaps you're right, perhaps he had no sense of history.'

'I become a little bemused trying to evaluate all this stuff.' I rubbed my eyes.

'You look it.'

'Today Clarence Cohen called me in for a chat. He's concerned that I'm not producing, that I've shown him no rough draft, not even a bibliography. I assured him that I've been researching constantly. But what! Frick has taken so much of my time, and then Berkman and Goldman. I've stopped short as I was starting to look at Carnegie. There seems to be virtually nothing available about Frick, only the Harvey biography. And still I've spent so much time with smatterings of contradictory evidence while the core of my studies has remained peripheral.'

'You're hung up trying to work out who were the good guys and who were the bad guys.'

'Perhaps that's it. Really, I think I've been caught up trying to find some truth behind the obvious. My studies have virtually become a ruse for this other thing. At times I even find myself flirting with admiration for Frick's energy. He was cocky in the face of reality. He set about reinventing the possibilities for making money quickly. In a sense his pursuit was totally amoral, a thing to be perfected for the glory of the chase. And then I concede that he probably believed in his task as a mission;

the captain of industry championing progress, playing his part in the development of his nation. Then I step back. After all what was the cost in human terms? Weren't Frick's social values in fact basically destructive and riddled with self-interest? Doesn't he end up wearing a black hat?

'But he continues to intrigue me. I suppose it's one of my basic assumptions that art has a civilising influence, that its record of human experience, its ironic commentary, its observing conscience, all influence human history. I rely on this, probably too much. Frick had such an eye for good art. I appreciate only too well that there's often a connection between art and money, between culture and affluence or power. But this man seems to have *understood* so much. It threatens me to consider that he may have known his paintings at their core, that his ruthless business acumen and his visual acuity may have stemmed from the same locus.'

'People are endlessly capable of productive hypocrisy. Why couldn't Frick have been a powerful capitalist, an art collector of discrimination, and a generous philanthropist at once?'

'Now you're sounding all too plausible, Steven.'

He let out a loud peal of laughter.

'For a Marxist, endless discussion is a major bourgeois stalling tactic: think what you like but don't, for God's sake, dream of doing anything.'

'And what about Natalie, does she engage you in heated debate?'

'She refuses to indulge me at all. She maintains that socialism is outmoded and discredited and refuses to discuss what she calls an extinct philosophy.'

THREE

At the end of the landing on the fourth floor of 187B 115th Street there was a window looking north. The fourth floor was occupied by the Fishbachs' two unmarried daughters who both worked as secretaries for the same Manhattan plastic bag manufacturer. At six forty-five each weekday morning a black limousine drew up outside the house. The two sisters, both in their early to mid-thirties, both small, delicate and slightly awkward in their movements, walked to the car and were driven away, not to return until after seven in the evening, in the same vehicle. During the week I developed the habit of taking a break from my research, which I was at last trying to focus, to walk up the last flight of stairs to the fourth floor landing. From the head of the stairs I could see the window, some ten metres away, first enclosed in its own frame, and then neatly framed by the tunnel perspective of the hallway. At the head of the stairs it was quite dark even in the middle of the day, and from this point the window acted on my eyes like a primary source of light. I often paused briefly, distracted by the intensity of the glowing rectangle of glass, before walking down the landing to look at the view. From the window there was a clear outlook over the rooftops and beyond the bay to the Manhattan skyline. I developed a familiarity with every mood of that cardboard cutout cityscape. The variations mounted like a carefully articulated series of paintings, recording changes in the time of year, the weather and the level of smog, which on some days obliterated the city in a turgid pall. Occasionally fog was so thick that the canvas remained a white plane, even the nearest roofs blanked out. As the winter deepened in the first couple of months of my stay at the Fishbachs' the number of blank days increased until the white was sometimes flecked and brushed with swirling snow.

It was at this time that I found myself adopted by another role. After Moishe moved to Brooklyn Elizabeth became totally emotionally dependent on me. A pattern developed; I went over to the house late in the afternoon and stayed all evening. Ruth and Herman vied for my attention insistently until their bedtime, after which Elizabeth and I spent hours talking. Whether we sat at the kitchen table drinking coffee and I ended up gratefully accepting cup after cup in an attempt to stay awake, or side by side on the built-in sofa, or lying in bed, our voices sounding frail and disembodied in the darkness, the conversation followed a repeated and repeated path. Why had Moishe left? Was Elizabeth such a failure for not putting that fatal pair of underwear in the drawer? Was she such an undesirable dog that the underwear had assumed such importance? Had she simply failed to talk to him? Had they both been subsumed in the cycle of living to such an extent that they had neglected their marriage? I said what I could again and again, intensely trying to imagine myself into this unknown situation. But, I confess, I had a recurring sensation that I was being bodily absorbed into instalment after instalment of an epic television soap opera.

It was also at this time that Herman returned home from the pet store on 109th Street with two rats in a cardboard box. He had already named them: Hambone and George. Ruth protested aggressively, but Elizabeth had no energy or will to resist the arrival of the rats. Ruth attempted to enlist Hannah's disapproval but Hannah, I noticed, ignored the fuss and spent most of her time in her room with the door shut. I helped Herman transform a tea chest from the garage into a cage while Ruth watched, making derisive remarks. For some weeks

Herman also spent much of the evening shut in his room. Ruth made sporadic attacks, bursting into his room hoping to find him doing, what she called, 'something nasty with those rodents'. To her glee she discovered him, after dinner one night, allowing George to lick saliva from his tongue. She dragged Herman down to the kitchen for what she hoped would be a major confrontation. Herman was quite relaxed about it all.

'George was real thirsty,' he explained to his mother placidly.

'Thirsty! Don't you know how gross that is you dirty little boy.' In Ruth's scornful tone I could hear an echo of Moishe at his most acerbic.

'It's not dirty.'

'It is.'

'It's not.'

'Rats live in sewers.'

'Not white rats like George and Hambone.'

'Rats carry disease.'

'Not George and Hambone.'

'You're a stupid, stupid –'

'Would you two be quiet and leave the room.'

'You're not going to let him get away with this!' Ruth stared at Elizabeth furiously. 'It's all your fault; since you and Dad split up Hannah doesn't talk to me and Herman has turned into a rat fanatic.'

About two months after Moishe's departure Elizabeth began to get angry with him. Her anger began with a series of complaints which developed into indignation at his behaviour, and then systematically and rapidly passed through periods of scorn, hysterical rage, loathing and finally into an even-tempered disdain. At times during this process I felt as though I would be swept away, as though the house would crumble before the force of her rage. Once, when we were talking late at night in my former room in the basement, she became so frustrated that she pounded at my chest with her fists while shouting: 'Why, why, why!' But this apparent desperation signalled Elizabeth's full return to her competent, active self. After a brief attempt at rebellion all three children willingly resumed their place in an ordered household. The only memorial to the period of Elizabeth's abdication were Herman's rats. He clung to them with such determination that she gave in, despite Ruth's mock horror. In fact, Ruth had become quite attached to George, who had learned to sit on her hand while cleaning his paws.

Elizabeth then began negotiations with Moishe over a divorce settlement and child custody. Many afternoons were spent in Moishe's office at the college, a number of them acrimonious. Elizabeth's lawyer advised her that until settlement I should not visit the house regularly and should never sleep there. She announced this to me in a businesslike way and I was surprised to find myself feeling hurt. I took up a regular life in my room at 187B 115th Street. Elizabeth visited me there late on most nights, and once or twice a week I went around for the evening meal with her and the children. In this way the anniversary of my arrival in New York came around.

Elizabeth's greeting kiss is the key to my memory of that night. She arrived towards eleven o'clock and her lips held the freshness of the freezing night air. Her cheeks were flushed and chill to my touch.

'Moishe rang me today.' I told her this as she lit the kerosene lamp.

'Really?'

'He asked me to have lunch with him next week.'

'Are you going?' Elizabeth was unravelling herself from her scarf and winter coat.

'Do you mind?'

'Why would I mind you eating with that bastard.' She had begun to undress.

'I've only seen him very briefly a couple of times at the college since he left and I thought –'

'There's absolutely no need to explain. I'm only glad it's you and not me.'

As Elizabeth undressed I considered, not for the first time, that her breasts must have been formed in conditions that did not promote the accumulation of fat. They were small and showed signs of having suckled three children. But now they made me smile, for they were quirkishly robust and perfectly suited to the woman they adorned.

'What are you grinning at?' she asked pugnaciously.

'Oh, just you.'

We embraced and then drew apart while I undressed.

'You know, you have cute buns.'

'Cute what?' As I spoke I guessed the meaning of this Americanism.

'What do you call them?'

'I suppose the nearest equivalent would be bum.'

'Ah, but then you can't admire them individually. I can distinguish between them – your left bun may be even cuter than the other one. You'd have to call them buttocks or something, which isn't at all the same.'

'Perhaps this is one of the few advantages of American English.'

'At last you concede something.'

As we made love I marvelled at the physical understanding which I felt had developed between us, despite my narrow, lumpy bed. It seemed astonishing that two human beings, wilful, self-conscious, even self-obsessed, could enjoy consummate intimacy. For a moment I gripped Elizabeth's waist in my hands and felt the extraordinary sensation that it was shrinking between them, vanishing to a thin wand of essential but vulnerable matter that I must cherish and protect or see lost forever.

While we rested, cuddled together, I looked at my small room. It was made quite romantic by the lamp-light. I listened to Elizabeth's breathing; she was asleep. Across the hall Dwight Rubour was playing 'Solitude' again and again. There came a point where the repetition almost ceased to be irritating. It became a given, a fact of existence. I caught myself listening, trying to compare various renditions in the sequence.

FOUR

The Island City–Brooklyn bus moved on one of the arcs of the four-leafed clover approaches to the Bay Park Bridge. I sat at the front, on the left side, where I watched the on-coming traffic. As the bus turned sharply I gripped the side of my seat, partly from a mild anxiety that the momentum of the turn would send us reeling into the Bay, but also simply to avoid lurching onto my neighbour who, that morning, was a particularly severe looking middle-aged woman.

I was travelling to the college to work at the library before going for lunch with Moishe, who had the afternoon off. The bus straightened and climbed onto the bridge. A police car approached from the other direction. I caught myself yawning without a hand over my mouth and was assailed by sudden guilt, by an irrational fear that one of the policemen in the car had seen me and that this somehow fundamentally compromised me. As the car passed, my sense of proportion reasserted itself. The bus was full of commuters who rode each day to Brooklyn, and on to Manhattan. We were crowded together in our heavy coats, scarves, hats and boots. Despite the intimacy of this physical situation most of the passengers steadfastly asserted their isolation, holding up books or newspapers or staring fixedly away from each other. A few mavericks attempted conversation over the unmuffled engine noise.

I got off the bus at the college exit and walked into the campus through snow which was already grey, even though it had fallen only the day before. Now the sky was a blue washed clear of its usual particles of urban grime. I stopped at a phone booth on my way to the library. The machine rejected my coins twice before connecting.

'Good morning, the Frick Collection.'

'Good morning, I've been trying to contact Ms Chapman, the curatorial assistant. Is she in this morning?'

'I'm sorry Ms Chapman is at a meeting. Could I take a message and have her call back?'

'Thank you, but unfortunately I'm not near a phone. I'll try again later.'

For several days I had been trying to speak to someone at the Frick who could help. I had decided to attempt to find more information. Ms Chapman's name had been given to me, but so far I had been unable to coincide with her. This, it seemed to me, was fundamental to the nature of telephone communication: non-coincidence.

At the library I settled down to work. I was looking, as a side issue, at those painters from the New York School who were born in the United States separately from those who immigrated. What were the differences of sensibility? I kept being diverted by such matters, and as usual time slipped by.

On the way to Moishe's office I tried the Frick again. This time the coins were accepted at my first attempt and I was put through immediately.

'Good morning, can I help?'

'Good morning, is that Ms Chapman?'

'Yes.'

'Thank you for sparing me a minute. I am working on a project regarding Mr Frick, and I wonder if you have any information available beyond the Harvey biography?'

'Have you been to the Frick Reference Library?'

'No. Could I have the address?'

'It abuts us. The entrance is on Seventy-first Street. Apart from that I don't know. There's nothing on Mr Frick himself here.'

After hanging up I felt a sense of anticipation. I imagined several shelves at the Reference Library stacked with folders of personal memos, newspaper articles, and perhaps, although this would have been out of character, a revealing diary. But now there was Moishe. Would he confront me, blame me, turn his scorn on me? I crossed the courtyard; the machine was roaring and there was no one in attendance.

Moishe was relaxed. As we drove he chatted freely, covering wide vistas of conversational ground with his usual ease. He was taking me to a restaurant in Park Slope with the unlikely name of The Bull and Thistle. The owner, Moishe told me, although a Brooklyn boy, was an Anglophile and had modelled his basically American diner on an English country pub. You could buy a ploughman's lunch. We swerved around a commercial van stopped in the middle of the street. Two men were bailed up against the van, legs astride, arms outstretched, guns at their backs, being frisked by policemen.

'If we have time after lunch I'll take you to my apartment; I think you'll like it.'

'You've settled in well?'

'It's just fine. Now that the kids are staying over a couple of nights a week it feels like home. It's entertaining watching them stake out new territory, organising their hierarchy and procedures; who sits where at the table, who does the dishes when. I guess you can picture it. And then there's

Herman and his box of goddam rats. How he slipped that one through on his mother I don't know. I tell him that diseases spread through the agency of rats have killed more people than all the wars and revolutions in history, but he is unimpressed.'

Moishe parked outside a restaurant called The Punjab Rose.

'Shall we eat?'

I got out of the car a little puzzled.

'What happened to our English country pub?'

'Didn't I say something? I suddenly felt like Indian food. Do you mind?'

Inside the restaurant there was piped Indian popular music. Each table had plastic roses in a vase full of water. We sat at a table under the front window.

'So, how do you think Elizabeth is doing?' Moishe asked, as soon as we had ordered.

'Much better now, I think.' I looked at him for some sign of his intentions but his face disclosed nothing.

'You know how I feel about my wife.' He paused, as though waiting for a reply. I was speechless. 'We've talked about how much she means to me a number of times.'

'Yes.'

'But now she seems to be rejecting me.'

'Moishe, what can I say?' Only as I spoke did the full impact of his words reach me.

'There's no need for you to say a thing. Elizabeth appears to have made a decision and I can't get through to her. When she asked me to move out I thought it would be for a short-term breathing space, a time for renegotiating some of the petty checks and balances of conjugal life. But now I wonder if I should have agreed to go. The thing I can't understand is that she has changed so quickly. This was the woman I knew so well, or thought I did, and now she seems to be somebody else.' Moishe's voice had a tone of slight moral disapproval mixed with bewilderment at some fundamental betrayal. 'Have you noticed a change in her?'

'This is hard for me, Moishe. In a sense I'm only just getting to know Elizabeth.' I hesitated, about to say more.

'I've never seen her so pushy, so demanding.' Moishe talked on about Elizabeth's transformation. I sat listening, myself bewildered by the course of the conversation. I had, at least, expected urbane resignation to the mortality of relationships from Moishe, and possibly a confident summation of Elizabeth's failings. I sat listening without saying anything more. The meal passed, the food unrecognised, unappreciated.

On the way back to the college our mood shifted. We stopped at Moishe's apartment. I helped him carry up some things he had collected from the house. He handed me a box of books. The box, made of cardboard, had 'FRESH BONELESS BREASTS' printed on the sides. I climbed the stairs, refreshed by the wonders of advertising English. Inside, Moishe showed me around, animating each room with an anecdote about the children. On the refrigerator there were several photographs, held on by magnets, of a man with his mouth wide open. I looked closer.

'That's you, isn't it?'

'Sure is. Hannah now has a craze for the back of my throat. Sometimes I worry that the kid has unhealthy obsessions. A few nights ago she started talking about the way people laugh, how weird it is that we open our mouths and reveal our wet, pink tongues and tonsils. I think that was how she put it. And then we let out those incredible bursts of noise. She immediately wanted to photograph me like I was laughing. She calls it a documentary project.'

FIVE

The day Hannah first came to visit me at 187B 115th Street, I had a flurry of other encounters.

Dwight Rubour spoke to me as we passed in the doorway. He was going out as I returned from shopping at Warburgs. He only greeted me, but this was a departure from the usual pattern of our chance meetings.

Milton Fishbach, possibly overhearing our voices, came out of his ground floor door as I was starting up the stairs.

'And how's my gentile Australian friend?'

'Well thanks, Mr Fishbach. And you?'

'Fuckin' terrible, God awful and lousy, thanking you. But who's complaining?'

I gave him the expected small chuckle. We had already had this exact exchange several times.

'Young man, let me tell you somethin'.' He walked right to me, planted his legs apart, leant an arm on the wall and looked up at me. Seen so close, in such clear focus, Milton Fishbach's face had an unnerving quality. The main features were animated, the mouth tauntingly sardonic, the eyes untrusting. But the physical impression of this head, the pale greasy skin, the large pores, was all but lifeless. Milton Fishbach's breath had a barren chemical odour, which I imagined was caused by the mixing in his stomach of several prescribed medications. 'Let me spell out a piece of good council. Eat right and if you can't keep away from women make sure they don't get pregnant. Let me illustrate. I ate what I goddam liked when I was young enough to think I'd live forever. And I drank the same way. Look at me now. My doc has me on this diet of baked fish and bananas. I ask you what's the fuckin' point? And I got married and had kids. Now I've got two grown daughters who want to spend all the money I spent a lifetime earning and who don't even have the sense to know what men have hidden in their pants. So they sit around at home, watch TV and get in my way.'

It was over half an hour before I extricated myself from this monologue.

Even at Warburgs I had been involved in conversation. In the vegetable section I noticed the man in the red and black lumber-jacket. Today, his footwear was thick black plastic fastened at his ankles with safety pins. One of the storehands was talking to him while sorting through a bin of apples.

'So bud, what do you think of Reagan?' the storehand asked him.

'Who?'

'Mr Reagan, the President.'

'Think of him? I don't think of him.'

The storehand laughed.

'You know, that's pretty funny. With delivery like that you could run for president yourself.' He noticed me as I passed. 'What do you think?' he asked me. 'Wouldn't this man make a fine president, or what?'

I smiled and nodded.

'I don't know,' said the man in the lumber-jacket. 'Am I old enough to run?'

Again, in the checkout line, I was accosted. A man touched my arm.

'Excuse me, sir,' he said in a strained voice. 'I wonder if you are interested in furthering your Jewish studies evenings. We are a serious group, several rabbis among us.'

'Sorry, but you're mistaken. I'm not even Jewish.'

'Oh,' he said, surprised, but also disapproving. 'I'm sorry to bother you.'

As he walked away I considered what he could have seen in me to suggest even a basis for rabbinical erudition. He was not stopping to ask other shoppers his question.

Later, after Hannah had left, after I had cooked and eaten, Steven visited me.

'I've brought a piece of popular culture to decorate your dull and refined quarters.' He unfolded a poster of a woman sitting astride a motorbike.

'It looks like an advertisement to me.'

'Exactly, as I said, popular culture. Advertising is the heartbeat of capitalism and of this country in particular.' When Steven's voice contained a sardonic element he sounded most like Moishe, but Steve's uncontainable enthusiasm made even his most cynical comments somehow fresh.

The woman in the photograph was wearing a black cap, and a tight, flimsy pink dress. Her visible thigh was pressed against the seat of the bike and her torso half turned towards the viewer. Her tanned left arm was raised and in her hand she held a golden, battered cylinder, some sort of fried fast-food. Above her head was the caption:

WHEN YOU WANT *THE* ROLL.

And under the photo was printed a brand name.

'Where will we put it up?' asked Steve.

'Well . . .'

'How about over your bed? I brought some tape, so we can complete the installation. I worry about you, kid, here in your studious bachelorhood. This brings a little commercial sexuality into your life. Look at the bike wheel rakishly turned towards us, like an invitation.' He sounded as though he were describing a particularly delicate flower or other natural wonder. 'Look at the girl's expression, that dress, her back arched to accentuate her breasts. And that deep fried thing, she's holding it at the correct angle of entry for her sexual organ.'

When the poster was duly hung over my bed I put the kettle on for coffee.

'Elizabeth asked me to say she'd love you to drop by.' I looked around from the stove. 'What's the matter Steve?'

Steven was looking past me, his face pale and tense. And then I remembered the gas cooker.

'I don't really feel like coffee do you?' I asked, as I turned off the burner. I remained facing away from Steven while I rearranged a few things on my tiny counter. When I turned around he looked composed again. 'Anyway, as I was saying, Elizabeth would like to see you.'

Steven smiled.

'You did that very well,' he said.

'Did what?'

'OK, we'll leave it alone, but thank you.'

There were a few moments of uncomfortable silence.

'You know, since you came over to see me that night I've been thinking about history. It's my mind, trivial as usual. It locks onto a sentence, a word, or moment and plays with it until tedium kills off its appeal. As you say, I like to speculate.' Steven's voice had changed slightly, was quieter, more relaxed. There had been a small breakthrough in our relationship. 'Anyway I started thinking again about Frick's moment in history and whether he understood it. You'll remember we discussed this. The other night I was standing in the kitchen, you have to understand the spasmodic way my head works, when I suddenly thought of Tolstoy's epilogue to *War and Peace* on history. For some reason it said, Look at me. I found reading it again interesting, although I'm not trying to make anything significant of this. *War and Peace* was finally published in 1869. Frick must have been a young man then?'

'He turned twenty that year. This was about the time he was starting to think about the potential of the coking industry.'

'You see, I just latch onto this sort of minor coincidence.

I may not share your obsession with Frick but I do get fascinated by the simple fact that these two people were inhaling and exhaling at the same moment in time. No, really. And there's the coincidence of their interest in Napoleon. I think Frick basically modelled himself on Napoleon – Rembrandt was the hero of his mature years. Napoleon, man of power, decisive action and destiny; that surely is how Frick saw it. Homestead was his Russian campaign but he would win. And Tolstoy, for whom Napoleon was a puppet to the forces of history – for him Frick would have been a comic dupe, convinced of his own destiny while acting out an inevitable part in a minor play.'

'Perhaps you underestimate Tolstoy's compassion for even the most marginal of characters.'

'Ah, here we come back to humanism, don't we. What you're asking is that despite all the shit people lay on each other we should still care, have loyalty to our species. Sometime we could spend a few evenings discussing ethics.'

'Indeed we might. But let's go back a minute. If I accept that Frick was a dupe, I assume you mean he was a dupe to capitalism, a servile agent of an inexorable system he did not truly understand.'

'I couldn't have put it better.'

'But, you see, when pressure was put on him by the Republican party to compromise over the strike he refused point blank. From his sickbed after the assassination attempt he vowed to win regardless of whoever might intervene. To me this is Frick's personality, his ego reacting to challenge, from the biological imperative of his own survival and success.'

'Oh, I get the idea. Like the atom or cell is to physical science so the self is to social organisation.'

'If you like. Capitalism is so resilient simply because it sits easiest with the selfish ambitions of the individual.'

'And socialism is always undermined, right? You know, we're starting to sound like each other.'

'Don't make me uneasy.'

As Steven was leaving I remembered to ask him something that had been flickering at the back of my mind.

'Steve, were you ill when you read *War and Peace*?'

'Ill? No. Why do you ask?'

'Oh, I was just curious.'

'As far as I remember I was a healthy young college student.'

And Hannah? I had not expected to find her at my door and, as though this initial dislocating second allowed me to see her differently, I was struck by her beauty. Hannah was now sixteen. Sometime over the last year she must have surreptitiously slipped from child to woman. I stepped aside to let her into my room and was momentarily unnerved by a sharp surge of lust as she passed me. What, I thought, was my relationship with Elizabeth doing to my hormones? Hannah sat down on the edge of my bed.

'Do you want to take off your coat?'

'Oh, thanks,' she said, standing up again. She took her camera from one pocket and an envelope from another, and then pulled off her coat, threw it on the bed and sat down again. 'I brought some photos to show you.'

'That's great. Would you like some coffee before we look.'

'Thanks.'

Now that Hannah was unswathed from her winter coat and the contours of her body were, according to Moishe's formula, more clearly defined, it occured to me that the sexual reaction I had just felt had been aroused purely by her face and stature. How incredible it was being a human being! Without any ritual encounter, without foreplay, or the display of sexual parts, or an emanation of erotic scent, I had become excited, solely by the most cursory contact imaginable.

'How do you like it?'

'White with one sugar.'

Hannah, when viewed dispassionately, was certainly far

more attractive than either of her parents. But, unlike her mother, who I was beginning to realise I might love, she was unknown. There was a cool, distancing cast to her expression which, until this meeting, had left her sexless, and even now made me uncomfortable as we attempted conversation.

I walked to the bed with the cups of coffee and sat down beside her.

'OK,' she said, taking her cup and putting it on the floor. 'I've been working on this project of images frozen at points where you wouldn't naturally be able to look at them for longer than a fraction of a second. I started out sitting around at Dad's apartment while everyone was watching TV. I had my camera ready, waiting for someone to laugh, or yawn, or sneeze or whatever. TV comedies worked best but it was pretty frustrating.' She showed me a number of photographs most of which were less than perfectly focused, but which still made a rather bizarre impression. One of Moishe was striking. He had his glasses off, held in front of him in one hand, his head was tipped forward, his mouth open obviously in laughter. But, in this isolated instant couldn't his expression, in fact, have been due to a sudden jab of pain?

'I got tired of this approach real fast. I decided to set things up. So, I got Dad to pose. This way I could set his head at any angle, with his mouth open any way I wanted, and get the camera right up close.'

The results were quite impressive. Hannah had saved and bought herself a new camera, a much more sophisticated instrument than her old polaroid. The photos were technically very good and visually interesting. But they had a peculiar quality, as though Moishe were somehow deformed or injured. And all he was doing was holding his mouth open.

'I'm impressed, but what are you trying to do?'

Hannah was silent.

'Don't worry if you don't want to talk about it,' I added.

'I thought you'd understand without asking.' She began putting the photographs back in their envelope.

'Perhaps I do, but this time I asked you first.'

She smiled.

'I'm trying to record something real about people's faces, something behind the everyday public face.'

'I see.' It interested me why Hannah should feel that a face with its mouth open, at a physical extreme, or even in a grimace, should be more real than a face in repose. The idea of symbolic dislocation was not new to me, but to Hannah? And it was her father's face alone that she was recording.

The conversation drifted on, moving more easily now. Hannah told me of Herman's latest craze, the rage of the last couple of days. He was trying to make explosives.

'That kid is real sick,' she said.

'Warfare, destruction, violence seem to be natural interests of the average nine-year-old.'

'Very funny. Herman is trying to make the bomb.'

'*The* Bomb?'

'Well, a bomb anyway.'

I thought, Well, A-bomb anyway, but restrained myself from comment.

'He has the equipment?'

'Oh, I don't know. He fools around with all this stuff in his room. Dad says it's educational.'

Before Hannah left she took numerous photographs of me and my room.

SIX

I was standing in the small entrance foyer of the Frick Art Reference Library. The uniformed doorman was on the telephone, relaying my request for admission. He got off the phone, had me sign in, and then directed me to the lift. A woman, probably in her late fifties, was waiting for me as the lift door slid open at my destination. Without any introduction, she led me into a large room, high ceilinged, quite sumptuously decorated and arrayed with handsome desks.

'This is the reading room.' She said this with a determination which denied the superfluousness of the description. 'Miss Helen Clay Frick set up the library after her father's death as a major repository for photographic documentation of art works for scholarly reseach. If you look at the painted frieze above us here, you'll notice the two cute dogs. These were Miss Frick's own pets, her favourites.'

My guide led me through the reading room, pointing out its various attributes, and then into an alcove lined with catalogue drawers. Here she began to describe the catalogue system in some detail. I took advantage of a pause to mention my own interest.

'I'm afraid there are no documents here relating to Mr Frick's personal or business affairs.'

'Nothing at all?'

'No, nothing.'

Back on Seventy-first Street I felt a rising level of combative frustration. Henry Clay Frick seemed to be consciously avoiding me, the official biography intended to remain as the only record of his identity. I walked to Fifth Avenue and passed the facade of the mansion, which I could imagine mocking my expectation of some sort of revelation. I paused and watched the building as though for a sign. Of course, Harvey's style of writing did establish an unintentional ironic counterpoint. And there were the union histories undermining the facade. But counterpoint was not what I wanted. It was what I definitely did not want. I had hoped for something written by the man himself, with no publication envisaged, a purely private document which might have disclosed some core of truth. Not an absolute truth, merely a clear and simple, even minor, demonstration of who Frick was. But would an ostensibly private document have been free from an inferred audience?

I walked down Seventieth Street to the entrance of the building. The rhythm of coming and going visitors, the pulling on and off of coats, the click of the turnstile, the loud voices coming in off the street while those leaving the museum were subdued; all this lent the foyer of the Frick a quality of familiarity and permanence.

In the shop I found the same young woman behind the counter as on my last visit. Her hair was again freshly washed. I asked her if Ms Chapman were in. She made a phone call, and informed me that Ms Chapman was not at her desk, but would, in fifteen minutes, be giving an introductory talk on the collection in the lecture hall.

I walked through the central courtyard pleased that my search might have another step to appease what had become a matter of pride, of contest. I checked my watch and decided to have a quick look at the Rembrandt self-portrait.

The gallery was empty except for an elderly couple at the other end and a guard standing midway along the wall, his hands behind his back. I stood in front of the painting almost feeling that this was a real confrontation. Rembrandt, or rather his own record of himself, looked back at me. But, of course, this was impossible. At most this image could assert itself before me. I looked at the face. It was painted broadly, almost loosely, yet the total effect was incisive. What had Frick seen in it? What had he seen in the man he wanted to be? Certainly Rembrandt had been a shrewd, even slick, businessman himself. But he had failed miserably finally, at least in business. Would Frick have admired that? There was a small red dab of paint on the right cheek. Had Frick ever considered that spot? It seemed to me that this touch of red, and every other stroke of paint on the canvas, individually, and when gathered together to make the self who had painted them, was evidence of vulnerability through knowledge.

I retraced my way to the lecture hall. People were beginning to file in.

The telephone picture I had formed of Ms Chapman was quite different from the woman herself. Her voice had suggested a businesslike person, perhaps in her mid-thirties, pleasant enough but authoritative. In fact, Ms Chapman was of small stature and appeared to be very young. Her hair was drawn back, her face clear and fresh. She stumbled several times over her words while delivering the lecture. I listened to the familiar information related this time from the perspective of the curators of the art collection. There were, though, two minor disclosures. A number of paintings in the collection, among them Ingres's portrait of Madame d'Haussonville, were bought after Frick's death. So much for my speculation over Frick's relationship with this painted woman. And the building itself was substantially altered after Frick died, including the transformation of the carriage court into the present garden courtyard. That Frick never knew this part of the building destabilised one of the few assumptions I had allowed myself about the man. I had imagined him sitting there at the centre of his domain, listening to the fountain, when he had never known it, when he had ridden across the court in carriages, or his fast automobiles.

At the end of the talk I went forward and introduced myself.

'Oh yes, I remember,' said Ms Chapman, guardedly.

'I'm sorry bothering you again, but I couldn't resist a final attempt to get information. You see, the Reference Library has nothing.'

'What is it you're looking for exactly?'

'Anything about Frick, particularly any primary material. Harvey hardly discloses a real human being.'

'Miss Frick directed the biography. She chose Colonel Harvey herself.'

'Colonel? I didn't realise he was a military man. Perhaps that explains his butchering of the language.'

Ms Chapman smiled. Only then did I notice how dark the skin was below her eyes.

'Look, there are a couple of articles I may be able to photocopy for you; nothing first-hand I'm afraid.'

'Anything would be wonderful.'

'OK. I'll meet you in the foyer in half an hour.'

'May I take you to lunch?'

She frowned slightly and then looked at me as though evaluating something.

'Alright, thank you.'

We sat in a diner on Lexington Avenue famous for its collection of teddybears, or so Ms Chapman told me. Certainly, there were many bears displayed in the window.

'Should I question the motivation for your curiosity about Frick?' she asked.

'I'd have to call it an ongoing fixation.'

'Different strokes.'

'I beg your pardon?'

'Oh nothing. I'll just have a piece of chocolate cake and

coffee, thanks.' She had been looking at the menu while we talked.

'I'm still impressed by you Americans, by your ability to go straight for hard-core farinacious foods without even a gesture to traditional eating habits.'

'Farinacious?'

'Sorry – rich, starchy.'

'And sweet?'

'Well, that's the lifeblood, isn't it?'

'The soul. You're Australian aren't you?'

'You're the first to guess it, Ms Chapman. Everyone thinks I'm English or Canadian.'

'Please, my name is Madelyn.'

Madelyn. The name perfectly suited her attractive girl's face with its tired eyes.

'So,' she said, 'what could possibly cause a young Australian to fixate on H. C. Frick?'

'Don't fixations evade logical explanation by nature? But that's quite a question from a worker at the Frick Collection.'

'Furthermore, I'm a communist.' She said this pertly.

I couldn't resist laughing.

'Not an anarchist? You can't imagine the pleasure that gives me. It ameliorates just a little what appears to be Frick's victory over my pursuit of him.'

We talked for some time about the tenuous position of communism in American political life, and then returned, by way of Berkman's attack, to the Harvey book.

'I mentioned that Helen Frick directed the biography. She actually related most of the information herself.'

'Is she still alive?'

'Oh yes, very much so. Ninety-four years old, I think. She adored her father and is obsessed with him, I'd say to the point of craziness. She has maintained the family house in Pittsburgh and kept it staffed and running like a Victorian household.'

'What house is this?'

'Clayton. Frick bought it shortly after his marriage. The

family lived there over twenty years. They only moved to New York because of Pittsburgh's industrial pollution. Frick was worried it would damage his art collection.'

We sat smiling at each other in complicity.

'The biography doesn't even mention the Pittsburgh house, except by inference,' I eventually said.

'I haven't seen the place myself, but I have seen a comprehensive series of photos taken by Childs Frick at the time the family lived at Clayton.'

'Who the hell was Childs Frick?'

'The only son.'

'I've never heard of him.'

'Oh well, Harvey was discussing the man and his place in history. But Frick was quite a family man in his own way. In photos his wife, Adelaide, looks like a sensuous woman in a proudly chaste kind of way. When their daughter, Martha, died – I think she was four or five – Frick was shattered. He called her his Rosebud and had her portrait engraved on his cheques.'

'I hadn't heard of Rosebud either.' I was smiling.

'You seem to have missed a lot. Frick even considered that Helen had an intellect. Apparently he used to discuss business matters with her.' Madelyn looked at me and laughed. 'They had one great falling out, over her coming-out party. Frick wanted his daughter to be received by New York society. She wanted to be with her friends in Pittsburgh. He stolidly refused to have anything to do with it . . . until she sent him an invitation with a plea written across the front. He came to the party. Are you getting any more of a picture? My God, how did I get started on all this? Anyway, I was telling you about Clayton. I believe the place is unchanged. Frick could walk back in tomorrow and feel at home. All the furnishings are intact. His clothes still hang in the wardrobes. There are photos on his desk, letters in the pigeonholes. His pills and medicines remain in the bathroom medicine chest. I also believe that virtually every note, bill, letter or other scrap of paper that passed through that house is preserved in the Archives in Clayton's old carriage house. But,' she said quickly as though to forestall my reaction, 'Miss Frick will allow none of it to be looked at.'

So, this was the denouement. I was to be tantalised and then sent away like the cheeky boy I probably was.

We talked on, but I had lost my usual concentration. I toyed with my lunch. I watched Madelyn Chapman's face. She described her work at the Frick. Apparently the upper floors of the museum where the staff worked suffered from peeling wallpaper and paint. When we parted outside the diner I thanked her genuinely, despite my flattened mood.

On the train I glanced at the photocopies she had given me. They were taken from various articles in *Apollo* magazine, May 1971, and from the introduction to *Masterpieces of the Frick Collection* by Harry D. M. Grier, an out of print book published in 1970. I read a little from the Grier introduction:

> The official opening of the Frick Collection . . . was greeted by a chorus of critical praise, not only for the excellence of the works of art and their setting, but also for the precedent established in art philanthropy . . . Since the opening more than five million visitors have come to the Collection from the United States and all parts of the globe; the attendance in recent years has averaged more than eight hundred a day.

Francis Poulenc was quoted:

> . . . of museums, the one I love best in the whole world – and I have visited many – the one that gives me most joy, is the Frick Collection in New York . . . Since I have a visual memory it is this museum which has comforted me . . . those beautiful paintings and the extraordinary building which houses them.

That was enough, I thought. But, as I was folding the papers in two, so they would fit in my coat pocket, I noticed handwriting scrawled across the back page:

The Archivist,
Frick Art Museum,
7227 Reynolds Ave.,
Pittsburgh, 15208.

This is just in case Helen Frick eventually dies before you do. Best wishes, Madelyn Chapman.

SEVEN

The Feinbaum children, like those of so many separated couples, enjoyed an historically unusual privilege. They lived what might be called a stereoscopic family life. Their parents were now strictly independent, except for being tied back to back by their concern and responsibility for these children. The kids moved between their two households, shifting behaviour patterns, sometimes glibly, sometimes with pain, but also watching both their parents, who less and less had any real picture of each other.

From the point of view of Hannah, Ruth and Herman the Island City Feinbaum household always had existed, of course. But now their father was not there to wrangle over what was played on the stereo, what was bought at Warburgs, who would sit where when watching what program on which television. Yes, Elizabeth had bought a colour television. It was an act of open rebellion in the early stages of her anger with Moishe.

Although Elizabeth had quite quickly re-established order in what had been a disintegrating household, the old checks and balances, the rituals and continuities were fundamentally altered. At night, seen from the street, or from the feathered needle tips of the pine trees, the house once again opened up in cross-section, its internal divisions made transparent, the members of the family would most likely be found dispersed. Ruth would be beating savagely at her drum kit, or locked in the bathroom engaged in some unnamed project of teenage self-beautification. Herman would be active, moving from watching television to hammering something in the basement, stopping in the kitchen to ask me to play cards, or bouncing a rubber ball on the stairs. Elizabeth would be unpacking groceries, cooking, sitting down to chat with me, or talking on the phone with Moishe in one of many long, unproductive, angry conversations. And Hannah, where would she be?

Hannah sat in the living-room. She was telling me about a car accident she had seen in Brooklyn that morning. The room was now spare: Moishe had half the furniture. Behind Hannah the bookshelves were nearly bare. Elizabeth had placed a basket of shells and a bowl of flowers on one of the shelves. Ruth was upstairs drumming, Elizabeth and Herman were at his school parent-teacher meetings.

'After the smash the traffic kept flowing past. There were car parts lying in the street and people just drove around them. I think I got some good pictures.'

'No one stopped?'

'Nobody. Not until the police came. Then a small crowd gathered; once it was official.'

'Was anyone hurt?'

'There wasn't any blood. So the crowd dispersed.'

I found it hard to tell whether Hannah was being cynical or merely matter-of-fact.

'I'm going for a walk on the beach, do you want to come?'

'Thanks, I'd like that,' I said.

The beach at night had unexpected qualities. Indeed, the Island City beach frequently surprised me. The first time after my arrival that it snowed I ran to the ocean. Australian beaches are synonymous with sunshine, by legend if not always in fact. But here, sure enough, the sand was covered in deep drifts, white right down to the breaking surf. And when the storm cleared, and the sun shone again, the deep grey green of the ocean met a dazzling line of snow. At night it was the proximity of suburbia, the lights left on over back doors, shining out onto the sand, the gleam of television sets through windows right at the edge of the beach, which was new to me. In the distance the curve of the club foot of the island was illuminated by lines of electric lights flickering and rippling, due, I supposed, to some property of the power current.

'Dad calls it the Doppler effect,' commented Hannah, when I pointed out the shimmering lights.

We walked near the water, which was sliding calmly up and down the gentle slope of sand. I looked for floating waste but the wash seemed beguilingly flat and clear.

'How are your photos of your father's head going?' I could see her face quite clearly in the light cast from the houses.

'I gave that thing up.'

'That doesn't sound like you.'

'Oh, I don't know. I tuned into the fact that Dad was having a great time making faces for me, or at me.'

'I see, he couldn't resist joining in.'

'Something like that. You know, there's something you ought to be told.' Hannah paused and stood looking at me. I noticed her breath coming in an even white stream on the cold, still air. 'My dad is seeing Natalie.'

'What do you mean?'

'My dad is seeing Natalie Bush, Steve's wife.'

'Hannah, what do you mean *seeing*?' I felt incredibly clumsy but I staggered on, trying to define her use of English.

'What do you want me to say? He's screwing her, OK!'

'I'm sorry, Hannah. I didn't mean to press you –'

'You did damn well then.'

She began to walk again and after a moment I followed her, feeling extremely foolish. When I caught up, she turned to me.

'I knew you wouldn't cope with this.' Her tone was calm again, patient, not at all sarcastic.

'Please Hannah, without my bumbling interruptions, explain what is happening.'

'My father is having an affair with Natalie, it's that simple. But I thought you should hear about it.'

'Does Steven know?'

'He will soon, Natalie is leaving him.'

'How do you know about this?'

'He's been my father for sixteen years and she's been a family friend over half that time.' She paused, but saw that I was unconvinced. 'You adults think that kids are deaf mutes of subnormal intelligence. Children overhear and see more than enough to put together a history of their parents' lives.'

While she spoke a petty but insistent question formed in my mind.

'How long has Moishe been involved with Natalie?'

'I've been waiting for you to ask that. When I finally understood what was happening I began to think about that too. It has been for a long time.'

'A long time?'

'Yes, I found a letter written by Natalie, a love letter, written way before Dad left home.'

We continued to walk, for some time in silence. Thoughts leapt back and forward in my head, repeating themselves, developing, retreating; thoughts finally based in notions of morality. What had Moishe really done to Elizabeth? What did the culminating irony of my own behaviour signify? And Steven?

'Are you angry with your father?' I asked, eventually.

'Why? What would be the point?'

'Well, for leaving home without really saying why.'

'That's the way he is, the way people are. He wouldn't see it like that. He wouldn't admit that was why he left, anyway.'

We turned around and left the beach, walking back through the streets. As we neared the house I asked another question.

'Hannah, why did you tell me this?'

'You needed to be prepared; how do you expect Mom and Steve are going to react?'

EIGHT

Steam rose from the stove in Moishe's kitchen. A saucepan lid rattled as the steam spurted out in little hurried puffs. From the next room came the sounds of a television quiz show, and from the hallway Ruth's voice was spasmodically superimposed over the television noise. She was talking on the telephone. Occasionally the voices separated as though in dialogue.

'What did Marnie say?'

'OK, Delta Blue Flies, for ten points, define semiterrestrial.'

'Did her Mom say she could take it for the whole week?'

'Which of these six animals are monotremes?'

'She told me there was no problem, only she had to wash it first with this herbal lotion.'

Moishe and I were drinking beer at the kitchen table. Moishe was in a feisty, even aggressive mood. It was as though he wanted to argue with me, would have enjoyed a heated clash of our different temperaments. He was baiting me on the topic of America's political role overseas. While he talked he got up and put the saucepan lid on an angle so the steam billowed freely, quietly.

'Sure the US has got itself into a few military and political stuff-ups since the war, but this persistent idea that we are some sort of stupid bully, a big-footed clown, stumbling around the globe, pushing here, tripping up there; this notion smacks of envy.' Moishe pulled out the grill tray where steak was cooking. He loved meat, and his income allowed him to indulge the passion fully. In my memory the texture, the colour, the cooking smells of red meat are intimately bound with Moishe. 'We filled the void left by a battered Europe at the end of the war and the change caused resentment. But, as I see it, European culture and political institutions were revived and revitalised in this country. We were Europe's natural heir. And still our ass is kicked hard for our mistakes. Wouldn't it have been easier for us to withdraw and let the rest of the world go hang? You have to remember that we made New York and Washington nuclear targets by guaranteeing retaliation for an attack on Europe. It's rarely appreciated what this historically unprecedented step means.'

I had visited Moishe that evening driven by a compulsion which had surprised me with its force. Hannah told me earlier in the week that this was the day that Natalie was leaving Steven. As Moishe talked I watched him for some sign of the inner reality, for a scrap of evidence of the unfolding events of his life. It was as though I must test my own ability to understand. Surely Moishe must show me something more than his mildly challenging conversational technique. Instead I waited, and finally engaged in his debate.

'A case could be made that it's in the American Administration's interest to back Europe and that, in fact, in a nuclear age there's no alternative as long as your policy is to oppose the Soviet Union.'

'And if we don't oppose them their influence spreads.'

'Exactly, until you're confronting Russia on your door-step instead of in Europe. In all this paranoia you have to remember that Russia has been invaded by the West three times in less than two hundred years; Napoleon in 1812, the Western allies in 1919 and by Hitler in 1941. Why should they trust the West?'

'So there's mistrust on both sides. But you're getting away from my point that our allies resent us.' Moishe had drained the pan and was now mashing the potatoes it contained. He paused in his beating and added a large spoon of margarine and a sprinkle of salt. He yelled out to Hannah, telling her to set the table. This was another of Moishe's characteristics, shouting instructions, requests, commands from one end of a building to the other.

Before the family sat down to eat I excused myself. Moishe walked with me to the door. Herman and Ruth were watching the television. It was a big, new colour set.

'You've capitulated to the pressure of modernity?' I asked, playfully.

'Not at all, it's a tactical move. Elizabeth got one and I can't let this place seem to be second class. I'm not going to lose my children.'

I stood for a few moments in the entrance hall, genuinely startled by Moishe's reply.

A key turned in the front door, it opened, and Natalie entered the room. She was dressed professionally, in skirt and jacket. Her blouse had little frilly things around the buttons. I imagined Moishe's hands inside the blouse, grasping Natalie's breasts, and my confusion was compounded. Natalie, too, was awkward in greeting me. After a few minutes of superficial conversation, which acted as a bridge between the old order of reality and the new, I left.

I caught the bus back to Island City, all the way thinking about Moishe. I repeatedly replayed my conversation with him at the Indian restaurant, replayed his tale of rejection. Moishe's actions and opinions had always seemed so deliberate, so self-conscious. Somewhere there was a major fracture in the consistency of related facts. But where did this fracture begin? Had Moishe so calmly manipulated events? Perhaps the fracture was somewhere else. I had been so blind, even now I might be missing the point. I felt a sudden rush of panic. Could Elizabeth have used me to rid herself of Moishe? But that was nonsense, must be nonsense. I felt tired and my throat tickled as though I were starting to get a cold.

Still I was pushed by a sense of the inevitable unfolding of events. I got off the bus at Steven's block and walked to the house.

'I didn't expect to see you today.' Steven said this as he stepped aside to let me in. What did he mean? I silently followed him to the kitchen. In one of those shifts of perception that continually catch me off guard, the house looked distinctly different. In fact it was unchanged, but now seemed sterile rather than stylish, barren rather than spare. I discovered my arrival had interrupted Steven while spreading cream cheese on a bagel.

'Have you eaten?' he asked brusquely, returning to his bagel.

'Steve, are you alright?'

'Me? Oh, I'm just great, fighting fit, never been better, more sprightly, more at one with the universe.' He went to the refrigerator and took out a bottle of white wine, slamming the door so that everything rattled and clashed on the shelves. 'Today is the day that you and I might constructively indulge in a discussion of ethical matters, the basics of human morality. Today Natalie has left me to pursue a sexual liaison with my best friend.'

'Steve, I am sorry.'

'Sorry? You have the nerve to talk to me about sorrow. Perhaps, if you hadn't been fucking the ass off Moishe's wife, he might have left mine alone.'

up in bed and leant on my elbows. 'How's everything, anyway?'

'Life goes on. I had a memorable appraisal today. The owner of the house, a man, was clothed and respectable but he had a pig in his living-room.'

'A live pig?'

'A real farmyard sow. He told me she weighed two hundred and something pounds. There was shit all over the carpet. I found it hard to believe he was serious about the sale.'

'Elizabeth, I feel delirious enough without your stories undermining my sense of proportion.'

'I also saw Steve today.'

'He visited you?'

'No, I went there.'

'How was it?'

'Terrible. I feel so guilty about him.'

'It's incredible, we go through all this and now, when Moishe and Natalie act, we feel guilt.'

'Are you suggesting we should have felt guilty earlier?'

'I'm not suggesting anything. I just think it's ironic we both blithely betrayed, excuse the melodrama of the word, betrayed Moishe. And now that we know he was lusting after Natalie long before that, we feel guilt.'

'If only none of it had happened.'

'If only your aunt had balls she'd be your uncle.' I tried to put my legs over the side of the bed. 'Excuse me, I have to piss.'

In the lavatory I felt decidedly shaky and leant one arm against the wall. I was weak but also shocked and angry.

Elizabeth watched me walking back to bed.

'Should I take you to a doctor?'

'Thanks, it's only a bad flu. I should be able to ride it out pretty well.'

Two weeks later I was still sick. I tried to get up several times, but putting on clothes was a major operation requiring total concentration. I felt completely without strength or energy. Elizabeth took me to a clinic at Kings County Hospital in Brooklyn. The nurse who took my blood for tests told me it was the biggest hospital in the world. In the several hours I spent waiting I saw no white person. My doctor was Indian, an affable but tired-looking man who remonstrated with me over the decline in Australian cricket. He suspected I had hepatitis.

After a few days the clinic telephoned Elizabeth and told her I was suffering from 'infectious mononucleosis'. I had never heard of it and found the term alarming.

'What's that to the lay person?'

'Mono, you've never heard of mono?'

'Whooping cough, diptheria, even the bubonic plague are vaguely familiar but not mono. Well, is it serious?'

'If you don't rest you could have it for months, possibly even permanently affect your health. It's an illness worth taking seriously.'

Eventually it was Moishe – he telephoned to see how I was doing – who told me that mononucleosis is glandular fever. Even in sickness there was linguistic diversion.

Elizabeth moved me to her house and into the bed she had shared for seventeen years with Moishe. In a show of domestic propriety she slept in the basement. The children, even Hannah, seemed to enjoy having me as a permanent, immobile inmate. I lay in bed day after day, studying every imperfection in the paintwork, too mentally inert to read for long. In that room I imagined the history of Elizabeth's marriage unravelling day by day from its first tentative moments, through its pregnancies, its nights broken by crying babies, its evolving sexual habits, its tenderness and frustrations. Once I asked her, not with jealousy but curiosity, if she missed Moishe. She shrugged her shoulders and told me she had lived with him a long time.

'That's what I was thinking,' I said.

'Now I find him repugnant.' She paused and looked at me

clearly, almost challengingly. 'But I miss the man he was.' Her voice was now quiet, almost impassive. 'Somewhere, sometime he stopped including me. Life went on normally but there was a terrible gap.'

When the children were at school and Elizabeth at work, I lay on my back listening to the vast empty space of the house around me. Occasionally it emitted noises, not exactly creaks or rattles but unidentifiable small sounds. Once or twice there was a loud bang as though someone were shutting a door downstairs, but no one came in. Many afternoons my fever rose to a level where controlled thought became tenuous. Things came and went through my mind.

I remembered being in the city, midtown on the East Side, and walking down a busy street. There was a truck double-parked. Men were milling about.

'The keys are in the trunk to boot,' shouted a thickset man wearing tight blue jeans. A helicopter passed overhead, following the line of the street. Horns began to sound as cars backed up behind the truck.

'The keys are in the trunk to boot,' I repeated the strange sentence to myself. It made a sort of sense, but it was an unusual thing to hear in the street. I passed under some scaffolding. Ahead of me stood a woman holding a briefcase, talking to two men. I recognised her.

'Ms Chapman, Madelyn,' I called out to her.

She looked around.

'Ah, it's you. Come with me, I have something to show you.'

We rode in a taxi to a hotel, the Waldorf-Astoria. She led me into the foyer. I felt disoriented by the bustling activity around us: travellers coming and going from the elevators and clustered around the reception desk, uniformed porters carrying bags, drinks waiters carrying trays. A boy passed calling someone's name for a message. All this reminded me of a scene from a familiar movie that I could not place.

'Ms Chapman – I'm sorry, Madelyn, I've been wanting to ask you, why do your eyes seem so sad?'

'Look,' she said, as though she had not heard me. 'Look over there.' She was pointing to an elderly man wearing the hotel uniform who was carrying two suitcases towards the main entrance.

I ran after him.

'Excuse me, excuse me please.'

He stopped and looked around at me.

'Is there something I can do for you, sir?'

I stood staring at the stern, distinguished face, the trim white hair and beard. But the beard might also have belonged to a well kept Father Christmas. Indeed, there was something patérnal about the face and gentle about the mouth and slightly drooping eyelids.

'Mr Frick?'

'Pardon me, sir?'

'Mr Frick, there are questions I have to ask you.'

'Excuse me, sir, there must be some mistake. My name is Bergman, Alex Bergman.'

During the weeks of my convalescence I thought a lot about Sasha Berkman, gradually more coherently. There was something about the naive fervour of his obsession that interested me. Perhaps it was his clarity of purpose. I admit I found myself comparing it with the determination behind Frick's every decision. But Berkman's life had, in a sense, had one moment. That moment had, of course, not quite worked out as he had wanted. Then the machinery of state punishment removed him from contention as a living being. Had his moment been successful, his removal from life would have been immediate and complete. And, of course, there would have been no Frick Collection. And my stay in New York? I let that speculation drift. When I started reading again Elizabeth brought me all my papers. I re-read Berkman's first letter to Emma Goldman after being released from solitary confinement.

From the hospital. Just out of the strait jacket, after eight days.

For over a year I was in the strictest solitary; for a long time mail and reading-matter were denied me . . . I have passed through a great crisis. Two of my best friends died in a frightful manner. The death of Russell, especially, affected me. He was very young, and my dearest and most devoted friend, and he died a terrible death. The doctor charged the boy with shamming, but now he says it was spinal meningitis. I cannot tell you the awful truth – it was nothing short of murder, and my poor friend rotted away by inches. When he died, they found his back one mass of bedsores. If you could read the pitiful letters he wrote, begging to see me and to be nursed by me! But the Warden wouldn't permit it. In some manner his agony seemed to communicate itself to me, and I began to experience the pains and symptoms that Russell described in his notes. I knew it was my sick fancy; I strove against it, but presently my legs showed signs of paralysis, and I suffered excruciating pain in the spinal column, just like Russell. I was afraid that I would be done to death like my poor friend . . . I was on the verge of suicide. I demanded to be relieved from the cell, and the Warden ordered me punished. I was put in the strait jacket. They bound my body in canvas, strapped my arms to the bed, and chained by feet to the posts. I was kept that way eight days, unable to move, rotting in my own excrement. Released prisoners called the attention of our own new Inspector to my case. He refused to believe that such things were being done in the penitentiary. Reports spread that I was going blind and insane. Then the Inspector visited the hospital and had me released from the jacket.

I am in pretty bad shape, but they have put me in the general ward now, and I am glad of the chance to send you this note.

'. . . and I am glad of the chance to send you this note.' I mouthed the words again. During his prison term, except in solitary confinement, Berkman was allowed to write one letter a month, on a single sheet of paper. On it he wrote up to six diminutive letters in minute but absolutely clear handwriting. The recipient of the letter carefully cut it into its parts and mailed them on. There were, I thought, things we took so much for granted.

There was another part of Goldman's book that I re-read.

In 1901 President McKinley was shot by Leon Czolgosz. The police immediately claimed the assassination had been incited by Goldman. She was arrested, interrogated, and on one occasion a police officer punched her in the jaw, knocking out a tooth and covering her face with blood. Eventually, due to lack of evidence, she was released.

Goldman had met Leon Czolgosz several times but the contacts had been superficial and he denied that she had any part in his act. Characteristically she decided to try to secure the young man a fair trial. The attitude of the press was hysterical. Although Czolgosz had acted independently there was a police hunt for anarchists throughout the country. A sympathetic guard sent out a message that Czolgosz had been repeatedly beaten into unconsciousness. No attorney could be found to act for him. Not even in the radical community would anyone speak out for his rights. Eventually two lawyers were assigned to his defence by the court. They publicly apologised for having to plead his case. Czolgosz had to be supported in court by two policemen, his head bandaged, his face disfigured.

Leon Czolgosz was strapped in an electric chair less than two months after McKinley was shot. While the executioner waited, his hand on the switch, a warden whispered:

'Leon, my boy, why do you shield that bad woman, Emma Goldman? She is not your friend. She has denounced you as a loafer, too lazy to work. She said you had always begged money from her. Emma Goldman has betrayed you, Leon. Why should you shield her?'

There were several seconds of silence.

'It doesn't matter what Emma Goldman has said about me.

She had nothing to do with my act. I did it alone. I did it for the American people.'

Seconds more of silence. Then there was a sizzling sound and the smell of burnt flesh.

Outside spring was asserting itself. I could see its developments in the neighbouring gardens from the window, simply by leaning forward a little in bed. The fresh green shoots seemed inappropriate, almost obscene. But how else was there hope of a process of healing?

As my appetite returned I thought of Berkman, who, when he was released from prison, ate almost as a substitute for all he had lost or could not face. He had been starved for many years, but now he consumed extraordinary quantities of food. He would follow a large meal with a dozen blintzes or a whole, huge apple pie. I felt some sort of identification, self-indulgent I know, as I walked down the stairs in my dressing-gown for a meal with Elizabeth and the children. I was still somewhat unsteady on my feet, but the thought of food was once again appealing.

I had plenty of time to watch the Feinbaum children. For over a month they were my major diversion. Hannah continued to treat me with a mixture of friendship, almost maternal condescension and aloofness. She often came and sat on the edge of the bed and showed me photographs. Herman had developed a comprehensive passion for explosives and their history. I discovered he did not attempt to make these weapons, only read about them and discussed them with his friends. He searched for the ultimate homemade bomb. He, too, sat on the edge of the bed. He described how ammonia crystals and iodine crystals, combined with water and then dried, produced a simple explosion on contact with a walking person; or how brake fluid and chlorine made a fine bomb. And, of course, there was gun powder, a combination of only three things: sulphur, potassium nitrate and carbon. As I watched Herman talking I kept having the bizarre hallucination that he was in fact his father, and that Moishe's career had taken a peculiar twist. And Ruth? She was preoccupied increasingly with herself and, in particular, with her hair. Once, when I knocked on the bathroom door before going in, Ruth's voice, sounding extraordinarily like her mother's, came from inside.

'Who is it?'

'It's me. Don't worry, I can wait.'

'I'll be exiting momentarily,' she said with reckless self-importance. Was this the same person who had opened her photograph album onto my knees shortly after my arrival in this country? Was this definitive evidence that I tended to overreact to inconsistencies? Perhaps the convenient inversions of the chameleon were, in fact, a natural part of the process of human growth and development? In any case, the changes in Ruth were clearly irreversible and, I knew, far from final.

Perhaps this was Berkman's real tragedy: his inability to adapt, his improbable sense of duty to an idea.

Frick had been equally uncompromising hadn't he? But his goals had been attained, had continued to be attained. The difference between the two men was that Frick had been shrewd enough to match his ambitions, considerable though they were, to the prevailing spirit, the existing conditions. What need had he to change or adapt? If there were a tragedy in Frick's life it was less apparent than Berkman's. But it was only less apparent because it was so normal, so familiar.

Some failures are so prevalent they can hardly be attached to the individual. Both Berkman and Frick had been the victims and perpetrators of violence. Violence was sanctified as the final solution. When discourse broke down, when points of intractable will were reached the solution was to smash the blockage. That was it. It was ultimately acceptable to kill people who did not agree with you. It was acceptable.

There was another outcome of my illness. I began to miss Australia. I missed family, certainly, but more than my life in town, much more than any cultural tie, I missed the landscape. I became nostalgic for the Australian forest. I developed a repetitive dream in which I walked under massive gum trees, peppermint, ribbon gum and brown barrel, thirty or forty metres tall, through an underbrush of delicate green grasses and bracken fern. Pockets of tree ferns reared fresh uncurling fronds, while dead, brown branches lay broken by their trunks. The air had a slight tang of fresh eucalyptus and rotting leaf mould. I breathed deeply and woke up.

TEN

'When do you think you'll leave?' Elizabeth was standing by the little window of my room at 187B 115th Street. While we talked she occasionally looked down into the neighbouring yards.

'I don't know. There's a lot to arrange.'

'It's not as though you have to sell a house or ship its belongings.'

I looked at Elizabeth. Her tone was hurt but it was she who

had made it clear that we would not live together permanently, or even for a more modest period. Sanity, she had told me, suggested that our age difference, her parental responsibilities, our cultural and national differences, her religious commitment, all led to separation. It was natural I should return home. I listened to her analysis calmly, but I understood that she was scared of something intangible. And, even though her announcement had struck at me painfully, somehow I shared her fear and felt a peculiar sense of relief, of escape. This intangible element, what was it? Perhaps it was in part a dread of rejection but also of commitment, of diminished possibilities, of a circumscribed routine with repercussions over many years. For Elizabeth, perhaps, it was the insecurity of a young lover, or wariness about the demands of a new relationship so soon after the old one. For me it may have been the responsibility of step-fatherhood or partly formed uneasiness over the boundaries of experience closing in around me.

Elizabeth was looking out the window. The sound of children playing in a schoolyard drifted to us across several blocks. Warm sunlight illuminated the scabby paintwork of the windowsill and the scratched vinyl tiles of the floor. It was summer; I was recovered and had been living back at the Fishbachs' for several weeks.

'Elizabeth, how long do you want me to stay?'

'When do you want to go?'

'This is ridiculous, you make me feel as though I'm trying to escape.'

'Aren't you?'

'That's hardly fair. You did suggest I should leave.' As I spoke I felt a twinge of guilt. Now that the decision was made I had become excited about returning home. And there was a growing feeling of relief that I would leave New York and its complications, which seemed to extend far beyond my personal life.

'Yes, I did.' Elizabeth's voice was quiet, expressionless.

'Have you changed your mind?'

'No.'

'Do you want me to plead with you to change your mind; to tell you that I want to stay?'

'Perhaps.' At last Elizabeth smiled and came across the room to me. We embraced. Looking over her shoulder at the sunlight on the floor I savoured the touch of her body against mine, the smell of her cheek, her hair. These things were real now, but would become increasingly inaccessible memories when I was gone. It was guilt which controlled Elizabeth's decision that I should leave. Her relationship with me had so perfectly parallelled the collapse of her marriage and friendships that I would always be a reminder of what she saw as her own failures. This, I now understood, was her nature.

ELEVEN

During the early stages of my illness Mr Fishbach and his wife had unexpectedly offered their help. They brought me cups of sweet, strong black tea, unrequested and prepared to their own formulation. No one in the Fishbach household drank tea but, thinking this was the sort of thing some foreigners did, they had bought a box of teabags at Warburgs. Milton Fishbach's monologues took on new qualities heard from the vantage point of fever. Mrs Fishbach, Myra, was quieter than her husband. She was a small person, her head disproportionately larger than her slight body. She set her own hair in rollers, often visiting me with a scarf or hair net on her head. Her hair was so thin that white patches of scalp were clearly visible between the curls.

When I told the Fishbachs that I would be leaving they seemed to be genuinely disappointed. They asked me into their living-room where we sat on chairs covered with protective layers of plastic. Milton Fishbach appeared to be incredulous that I should want to leave the United States. How did this square, I thought, with all the previous months of bitter and cynical attack on every institution and public figure in the country?

Clarence Cohen also was disappointed, even annoyed with my decision. It was not that I was such a prize student, but, in an era of shrinking graduate student numbers, any loss was unwelcome.

At the age of twenty-four I dreaded facing my parents. But when I made the call they sounded relieved that I was coming home. So my ticket was booked, for a Saturday afternoon late in September 1983. For the last week I moved back into the basement room in the Feinbaums' house. As I carried my suitcase down the stairs, I thought of the evening of my arrival. I stood in the doorway of my room; it was set up much as it had been then. I almost expected to see myself lying in bed reading, to see Herman and Ruth playing pool. Now the pool table was covered with things, cardboard boxes, a hand saw, a basketball, some clothes. I distinctly felt Moishe's absence. I could hear the rest of the family in the kitchen, talking, moving chairs, preparing for dinner. There was no jazz coming from the living-room, and no sound of the predominant surge of Moishe's voice calling everyone to attention, as it always did by implication. Quite irrationally I waited, listening for jazz. I felt a small rush of panic trying to validate my memory, as though I had never heard jazz coming from the living-room, as though jazz itself had never existed. But who had invented my memory of it? Had Moishe convinced me of its existence through words alone; had he reinvented history as an assertion of his own personality? I laughed aloud and continued into the room.

Moishe rang the house that night and asked to speak to me. I had not seen him since my illness. He suggested we have coffee on the morning of my departure. He would collect me at ten o'clock.

That Saturday morning all the children left the house early on private missions. Elizabeth went shopping to avoid seeing Moishe. It was planned that everyone would be back at midday for lunch, before driving me to the airport. So I finished my packing and sat down to read, and wait. I found it difficult to concentrate on my book. I began constructing possible versions of my meeting with Moishe. At eleven o'clock he had not arrived. Then the telephone rang. My immediate thought was that he was calling to say he was not coming.

'Hello?'

'Hello.'

'Is that you, Moishe?'

'No.' There was a pause. 'It's Steven.'

I was too confused to feel the full measure of my embarrassment.

'Oh, how are you?'

'OK. I thought I'd call to say goodbye.' There was another pause, while I struggled for coherence. 'I want you to know that I regret that I've denied myself your company over the last few months.'

'Steve, I really appreciate this. On my part, I'm sorry if I've contributed to your pain.'

'Whatever I may have said, we both know it had nothing to do with you.'

'I'm no longer so sure.'

'I think it's a good thing you're leaving. Don't get me wrong about that; I mean good for you.'

'Thanks, Steve.'

'This place is bad for you. The country is going down the tube, slowly, insidiously. If it happened quickly you could react. But it's so easy, it slips along carrying people of good will with it, numbed and dazed and quiescent.'

'You sound pretty depressed, Steve.'

'Don't worry about me, just get the hell back home.'

'Really, I wonder if Australia isn't on a similar track, just moving a little more slowly, a little bit behind.'

'Fuck it kid, Australia isn't a world power yet. Your generation, at least, should be free from the excesses of collective arrogance, collective self-importance, collective megalomania. Morally we blew it when we dropped the bomb, and killed off any vestige of hope with the cold war. Each new generation has been poisoned by the communal lie. We're a nation of dead people.'

'Steve, can I see you today? I've an hour.'

'I've got to go.' There was a pause. 'Good luck.'

'Steve, just a minute. I'm worried about you.' While I was still speaking I heard the nagging bleep of the disconnected line.

At the airport each of the children hugged me, even Hannah. Despite our attempt to deny the extremity of the situation, Elizabeth and I cried in each other's arms. And then we said goodbye.

In the aeroplane people crowded in the aisles searching for their seats, stowing their luggage. Stewardesses passed, smiling hurriedly on eye contact. The smell of stale air blew from the overhead vents. I sat thinking of Moishe. It seemed that my understanding of him had continued to diminish until this last moment.

PART **THREE**

ONE
REPLAY

Moishe, Steven and I were sitting in the Feinbaums' living-room. Our chairs formed the three points of an equilateral triangle. Moishe lounged in his armchair. His physical presence was absolute. Steven, tall and angular, was perched on a wooden rocking chair, his feet drawn up on its edge. Somehow he looked comfortable in his awkwardness.

I cannot see myself, cannot feel the chair, or is it a stool, on which I must have been sitting. I am only vaguely aware of my observing consciousness, as though it were hovering independently somewhere above the polished wood floor. I know I was watching my two companions but what was I thinking or saying?

When, several months after my return to Australia, I remembered this scene and the conversation which accompanied it, the thing about it that most preoccupied me was the intangibility of my own role. After reliving the scene many times I then attempted to place it in time and context. The conversation must have occurred during my first summer in New York. I deduced this simply from the clothes I recalled Moishe and Steven wearing and the sense of heat in the room. But I could not remember anything else about the evening, or position it between other events at that time. Yes, there were the obvious things. Moishe had talked, as only Moishe could talk, to Steven and me about adultery. But my memory had shut myself out like a protective mechanism.

It was exactly this hole in my memory which eventually pushed me to attempt to reconstruct my time in New York. My own fallibility caused me to reconsider the other frustrations of my stay in the United States. There was that other triangle, with Henry Clay Frick, Alexander Berkman and myself at its three points.

This pair of triangles is probably too tidy a conceit. Perhaps the pattern I was sure I saw, and wanted to understand properly, was more like a cluster of mutated forms, hardly geometric or simple. Room had to be made for the city of New York which, after all, animated and mystified my story, both public and private.

The selective nature of my own memory was clearly part of the pattern. I could see that now. I was hardly an objective instrument for recording the complexities of experience. All I had was my experience filtered through five or six years of my memory. And I had my own interests, had placed my own pressures on unfolding events. Disclosing a story I had actually lived was, if anything, more difficult than the familiar frustrations of public history. And here I had a complex hybrid to remake. But this, in itself, became exciting. History as a hybrid of the public and the personal became a compelling idea. An objective record seemed so improbable. It increasingly fascinated me that Frick and, for that matter, Moishe had deliberately obscured themselves. Or was it less intentional than intrinsic to character that both men had hidden themselves? Was the real geometry of this story found in a pair of parallel lines, very different looking but distinctly parallel lines. Yes, this would be the book.

So, my fixation with my own memory shifted in emphasis. And it was augmented by a sense of gratitude. After all, everything I had witnessed in New York was now part of my history. The intensity of the experiences, the rapidity of the process of exposure to new things, this was all a gift. And the people; how could I measure the value of having known them?

The plan to reconstruct my time in New York remained just that for several years. Reconstructing a life in Australia intervened. I abandoned any intention of further study and took a series of desk jobs unrelated to my training. I did not move back into my parents' house but rented a flat. I also embarked on a brief series of relationships with young, unmarried women. And I went bushwalking regularly in an attempt to flesh out the memories of south-eastern forest which had sustained me in Island City. I returned towardss the end of an extremely severe drought, and the bush was almost as dry and forlorn as the stereotypical view of Australia would have it. I was more surprised than disappointed. But I did keep hearing Moishe's voice: 'That was no place for people.'

In early 1987 I began making notes of my memories of the Feinbaum household and re-reading material on Frick. Catherine Green, my lover for the previous two years, suggested that we make a trip to New York together. So, we planned and saved, and left for a three-week holiday early in January 1988.

No one was waiting for us at the airport. Of the people I had known and written to, even Elizabeth, after a letter or two, had slipped out of my life. Only Hannah had written back occasionally. As the train to Manhattan left the station I felt we were travelling in the wrong direction.

For the next couple of weeks Catherine and I absorbed the mythology of the city. We even went to the top of the Empire State Building, something I had not done during my stay. The Frick was saved virtually until last. I liked to think it was being kept waiting. As it turned out Catherine enjoyed the Frick less than I had expected. She was not keen on the idea of the place, of paintings embalmed in a wealthy man's fusty living quarters.

We had a whispered argument in the courtyard. On the way out I went to the museum shop. There was a young man behind the desk. I asked him if Madelyn Chapman was still on the staff. He had not heard of her.

Ms Chapman's departure nagged at me. Back in the hotel I telephoned the Frick and asked to speak to her. I was put on to a pleasant woman who explained that Ms Chapman had left the museum a couple of years previously but asked if she could help.

'Yes, you can, actually. It may sound like a strange question, but I'd like to know if Helen Frick is still alive.'

'Miss Frick died in 1984.'

'Can you tell me if the Frick archives are now available for study?'

'Not to the public. I believe selected academics have been given access.'

After I hung up the phone I sat in my chair thinking. I was no longer really interested in the information itself, only its denial to me. I think this realisation shocked me, then. It was almost as though the possibility of ever seeing the material in the archives destroyed the symmetry of my frustration. What I had to understand was that the coincidence of my own life with the public record of Frick's was in the past. Now I was starting to write the story of this coincidence, but in essence, it was a story contained by the past. Anything I might learn now would be part, quite possibly, of another book. Still, at times recently I had been uneasy about the reliability of the research I had done. What had I missed? But this wasn't the point. I had discovered all I was able or inclined to discover at the time. That was the point. In any case, I suspected basically that Frick had been too careful to have let a thing slip. Or, if not careful, then constitutionally incapable of revealing himself. Wasn't it clear to me by now that the denial of information, the persistence of contradiction were at the core of this history?

I tried to telephone Hannah several times. The last address

I had was an apartment in the Nineties on the West Side. But that letter was written over a year earlier. No one answered the phone. Then, towardss the end of the second week, I got through. And it was Hannah. There were a few moments of mutual dislocation before we were able to talk coherently. I discovered that she was the only member of the family still living in New York. We arranged to have coffee together the following Monday, two days before Catherine and I were due to leave.

TWO
NOSTALGIA

Catherine and I were lying in bed. We were watching the hotel television. I had insisted that we watch a movie, one which we had both seen too many times already. It was *Casablanca.* I could not believe that it had been programmed during this visit to New York; and now I was lying beside Catherine's warm body, overcome with intense nostalgia.

The next day I took the subway and the bus to Island City alone. Catherine had wanted to stay in the city. I sat looking at the familiar Brooklyn streets, counting the stops to the university. The bay looked extremely cold and sterile from the Bridge, and Island City flat and colourless ahead. I got off the bus at 148th Street and walked to the beach. It was the same; the same as on any windy winter's day during my time there. The flat grey sand, the broken jetties catching the waves, the distant line of apartment buildings; it all filled me with intense loneliness. I walked along the beach looking at the houses. Blistered paint was peeling from many of the walls facing the Atlantic and the few trees in the gardens were twisted towards the houses, bent by the prevailing winds off the ocean. The place had a deserted quality, like a run-down seasonal resort, or, at least, a weekend community. I turned onto 137th Street without having met anyone on the beach.

As I entered the block on which the Feinbaums had lived I noted with interest a surge in what had already been my steadily rising level of nervous excitement. I walked along the uneven sidewalk in something of a haze and once tripped over a protruding seam in the concrete. When I saw the house I stopped. Immediately I regretted this attempt to recreate a memory. I walked closer, as if to verify that I was looking at the right house. The pine trees had been cut down. There was no sign that they had existed. A bed of azaleas and a neatly trimmed lawn stood where I remembered the trees. The woodwork of the house had been covered with blue aluminium siding. A blue and white striped awning with tassled fringe hung over the front living-room window. Ostensibly this was the same middle-class suburban street. 137th Street, Island City, New York. If you had passed this way only a few times you would probably notice no difference in its natural order. You would not know that one of the houses had been altered so that it did not retain the history of a family.

The next bus was not due for forty minutes – I still remembered the timetable – so I walked towardss 109th Street. As I neared 115th Street I decided to have a look at 187B. Why not? I had come this far. Reassuringly the building looked exactly as I remembered it. I stood at the gate for some time and then decided to go in and ring the doorbell. After a while I heard the inner door open and someone come out.

'What do you want?' It was Mrs Fishbach's voice, reserved, suspicious.

I told her who it was, adding, because I thought she may have forgotten my name, that I was the Australian lodger.

'I can't see anyone, I'm serving my husband lunch.'

I heard her feet shuffling back inside and the inner door close. I stood by the door mildly crestfallen. There was something bizarre here. This was like a scene from a dream where connected events draw near and then slide apart at the last instant, unresolved. I slowly walked down the front steps and along the path. I paused at the gate and looked around. Mrs Fishbach was watching me from one of the ground floor windows. We remained still, looking at each other. Then she tapped at the window, pointed towards the door and disappeared. I turned back, hesitatingly. The door opened slightly and Mrs Fishbach put out her head.

'I know you,' she said. 'But I didn't recognise your voice.' She beckoned to me to come in. 'I have to be careful of the muggers, you see.' I followed her into the hallway and into her sitting-room. She asked me to sit down. The room was as I remembered it except previously there had been a tall stack of issues of the *Wall Street Journal* beside Milton Fishbach's armchair under the window.

'How is Mr Fishbach?'

'Mr Fishbach passed away in the fall.'

'Oh, I'm sorry.' And I was. I could not have explained why I should regret the death of so negative a person. I wished I had seen him this once more.

'Don't bother. Milton was a son of a bitch. He had a nasty nature, used coarse language in my house, and didn't bring home a nickel.' Mrs Fishbach said this without emotion, as though addressing some minor conversational topic. 'It was better while he still worked. I had the day to myself. I did housework mornings and, once the girls were at school, had the afternoon to go shopping in Brooklyn. The shops were nice in the fifties, even the sixties. All of Flatbush Avenue was nice stores, dress shops, hairdressers, diners. Not like the trash now. I had lunch and saw a movie. I used to give my hair a grey rinse and make myself look old so I could buy my movie ticket half price. I always got in to see the movie half price.'

THREE **COFFEE**

I stood outside the café window and watched the passersby carefully. I wanted to see Hannah as she approached, I wanted time to absorb her physical appearance, to prepare myself for the meeting. I considered what I remembered of her. She was twenty now, nearly twenty-one.

When she did arrive, I noticed Hannah only seconds before she was standing in front of me. She was carrying a large black book. We greeted each other hastily. I kissed her cheek. She pushed the door of the café before I could open it for her.

Hannah greeted the staff of the café familiarly and took a table. As we took off our coats and pulled up our chairs, we continued the introductory process begun outside. So, how *are* you? Great thanks, and you? Hannah placed the heavy book by her chair. We ordered coffee and cake. Hannah took immediate control of the conversation. Talking quickly she told me of her family. Elizabeth was living in Boston. She remarried last year. A nice man. Ruth and Herman were with her. Ruth was in the last year of high school, Herman the last of junior high. I listened, feeling as though the intervening years were passing as she spoke. Moishe was at Ann Arbor. Yes, he and Natalie were still together, now married. They were married in a synagogue. In fact Moishe was now a regular at temple. This was Moishe! Were Natalie and Moishe happy? Yes. They fought; they loved to fight, but that was the status quo. And Steven Redman? No one had heard from him for a couple of years. He had disappeared.

A waiter brought our coffee. Hannah asked me about the trip. How did I like being back in the States? Another phase of pleasantries. I mentioned my visit to Island City. She became silent suddenly. I looked at her face. It was now the face of a mature woman, complete with every sign of adult consciousness. She was attractive but it was a beauty controlled by a healthy ego.

'You know, this may shock you, but I pretty much resented you being in our house.'

'I often wondered if you did.' Only now did it occur to me that this meeting might be more important to Hannah than it was to me.

'Don't get me wrong, I liked you, but I resented the fact you were so entranced with my mother.'

'I was entranced by your whole family.'

'I know you were my mother's lover.' Hannah watched me closely as she said this, waiting for a reaction. In fact, I was not surprised. I remembered her ability to unnerve.

'What would you like me to say? Should I offer an apology?'

'I'd like to know when you were first attracted to her.'

'You always surprised me, Hannah, by the details that interested you. Perhaps you recall the time you upset your father by discussing the intricacies of vomiting at the dinner table? I remember it clearly. You told us all that every time we throw up we empty our digestive tracts from the large bowel, up twelve feet of intestine, into the stomach and then out our mouths. You seemed so proud of this feat, or perhaps it was your knowledge of it. Moishe thought your fascination was an unhealthy fixation, and you put Herman off his food.'

Hannah remained silent, watching me.

'Look Hannah, I can remember details like that, but I can't retrace the exact path of what happened between Elizabeth and me. I'll try to be candid with you. When I arrived in your household I was pretty well removed from active contact with people outside the warmth of my own family. Your mother, you all, broke down my reserve, socialised me as it were. If I contributed to the breakdown of your family, and I don't know that I did, I can only say I am extremely sorry.'

'Don't pretend she seduced you. If you weren't actively pursuing her, you were at least waiting for something to happen.'

'That may be true. But you must see I'm not going to apologise for my relationship with Elizabeth. I can only apologise for any affect on you and your brother and sister.'

Hannah smiled at me.

'I had to give you a hard time.'

'Thanks a lot. Have I survived it?'

'Yes, quite well actually.'

There was a pause.

'And what about my father?'

'Moishe? What can be said about him? I have trouble fully comprehending who your father is.'

'You too. Do you believe I've really wanted to talk to you about this? I went to a therapist for nearly two years trying to understand my relationship with my father. And that was after not thinking about him at all for a long time. I thought about you now and again. It seemed to me that you might understand the problem.'

'I certainly appreciate it but, as for answers, Moishe still eludes me.'

'What about his time with your family? I think my father

brought back some sort of ideal he was never able to reproduce here.'

'He admired my parents but I don't know that they had such a profound effect.'

'Have you tried to measure the effect your stay here had on you?'

'I take your point.'

'Can you suggest a core reason why Dad might have idealised your family?'

'When I arrived here I immediately saw that he did try to emulate the closeness of our family life. My parents were unique, or at least very unusual. There was a sense of unpretentious civilisation in our house, of independence from contemporary pressures, of warmth, civility, of understanding.'

'Eventual failure number one.'

I looked at Hannah. She seemed to be elated, as though this were a game she knew she was going to win.

'There is something else, which may come close to what you're looking for. In everything my parents did there was a fundamental belief in their own ability to get results. This world could be evaluated, discriminating decisions reached, and changes made. There was no place for apathy. Listening to Moishe I sometimes got the feeling that he lived in the shadow of this clarity of purpose. It was implicit in his tendency to ironise his own place in the unwieldy momentum of New York life.'

'And you still think all this wasn't that important?'

'Well, I'm not sure it was *that* important.'

'Australia and your parents were different. They gave Dad something to distinguish himself from normal life. Sure, their attraction may have been incidental. I think my father would have inevitably found something to romanticise so he could fail to live up to it.'

'Hannah, isn't this all a bit plausible? What about the rest of Moishe's formative years? I know virtually nothing about his own family. I got the impression of a crowded Jewish household but I don't think he ever talked about it, except for the occasional apocryphal anecdote about his grandmother.'

'That's just it. Dad revealed nothing. It's funny, but my photography studies started off an attempt to come to terms with him. I was reading about the photographer Jo Spence. She ran a commercial photo studio from the late sixties to the early seventies. In that time she constantly took pictures of brides and weddings, family groups, portraits, all that sort of stuff. But she did not receive one father and child commission. This idea fascinated me. I went through every photo my family had, searched both my mother's and father's apartments, but I could not find one photo of my father and me alone together. This lack of any record obsessed me. You know how much time he spent with us kids. He liked to play at being our pal. But that was just it, I could not remember a single, sustained, intimate conversation with him. He liked to banter, to storytell, to lecture, but did he ever talk? It's almost like he never said a thing.'

Hannah reached down and lifted the fat black book onto the table.

'I have literally taken hundreds of photos of my father, trying to pin down something permanent, real!' She faced the book towards me and flipped through a thick handful of pages. Dozens of photographs of Moishe turned one after another.

'May I have a closer look?'

She pushed the book towards me.

'I'm going to the bathroom. Will I order another coffee on the way?'

'Thanks.'

I leafed through the book. Moishe was there in incredible strength, filling over half of it. Abdicating from any attempt to compare or evaluate this multi-faceted record, I simply looked at page after page.

'Crazy isn't it,' said Hannah as she returned. 'Do you know what I ended up thinking? I think Dad set us all up.'

'That's a bit paranoid isn't it?'

'I definitely think he set you up.'

'It was always a possibility, but, in the end, I doubt it.'

'He wanted you to get involved with my mother so he had an excuse to leave.'

'If that's so, then why didn't he make real use of my relationship with Elizabeth, make a fuss about it?'

'No, it wasn't like that. None of this was conscious. That's the basic thing about my father. He is intelligent, but he is totally unaware of his own internal workings. He is an urbane but very vulnerable man. There is no way he could ever admit any guilt. There is no room for fault in his self-image. He needed you to excuse himself. And he could not know he needed you.'

'No, Hannah. This is too transparent. I've toyed with similar thoughts, but your father is actually the most self-conscious person I've ever met.'

'OK, yes, conscious of the immediate performance, of his effect on people, his image. But his subconscious behaviour is totally reflexive. I've had a lot more arguments with him than you have. There is a yawning gap between the sophistication of his mind and his inner insecurity. He has a compulsive need to reinvent reality to suit his self-image.'

'But Hannah, his behaviour was always so quirkish, so inconsistent.' It was as though I wanted to protect my memory of Moishe from what might have been a clinically accurate dissection.

'Yes. Still, this is the view I've formed. It stands for now.'

We talked a while longer and then, as if at a mutually recognised signal, we rose and left. In the street we said goodbye. I stood and watched Hannah walk away. For a moment other pedestrians blocked my view of her, but she reappeared in a gap between moving bodies. Instinctively, I knew this glimpse of her was the last thread connecting my immediate experience of her, of her family, with memory. And then she was gone.

EPILOGUE

Several months ago, that is, towards the end of 1989, an attentive friend brought me a worn paperback copy of S. N. Behrman's *Duveen*, a biography of one of history's most ambitious art dealers. Since the trip back to New York I had been circumspect about mentioning the book I was writing, but, possibly because it was virtually finished, I must have let slip some reference to it. My friend gave me the paperback with the comment that Frick appeared in it.

Duveen's greatest success was the shipment of huge quantities of Italian Renaissance art from Europe to create the collections of America's new millionaires. He preyed brilliantly on the competition between these usually wary businessmen. They vied for immortality through the magnificence of the public bequests they would leave.

Behrman called one of his chapters 'The Silent Men' after Duveen's clients. They all shared 'a suspicion that talk breeds friendship and that friendship can be expensive . . . Once you have achieved some sort of human relationship with a man, it is hard to bring yourself to sell him a few groceries for half a million dollars.'

Frick was more silent than most. Although he was one of Duveen's major customers Behrman's book had little information about him, and most of that was taken from Harvey. But I did find several anecdotes which I immediately knew would provide me with this brief epilogue.

Behrman quoted a story told by the art historian Bernard Berenson:

Of all the important American collectors, Berenson admired Frick the most, it appeared. For one thing, he had a beautiful head . . . collectors of Frick's era, he said, often felt guilty about paying such vast sums for their pictures, and Frick was no exception. Frick had bought Velasquez's "Philip IV of Spain" for around four hundred thousand dollars. Learning that Philip IV had paid Velasquez the equivalent of six hundred dollars for it, Frick made an elaborate computation to find out what six hundred dollars at six percent interest compounded semi-annually from 1645 to 1910 would come to, and found, to his joy, that he had got the picture for less than nothing.

But another anecdote showed that Frick, too, became a victim of Duveen's marketing practices. Duveen bought several busts by the French sculptor Houdon at twenty-five thousand dollars. He then bid seventy-five thousand dollars for a Houdon at public auction. The world market followed his lead. Subsequently he sold Frick two of his Houdon busts.

Finally, Behrman described Frick at home:

It was Frick's custom to have an organist in on Saturday afternoons to fill the gallery of his mansion at Seventieth Street and Fifth Avenue with the majestic strains of 'The Rosary' and 'Silver Threads Among the Gold' while he himself sat on a Renaissance throne, under a baldachino, and every now and then looked up from his *Saturday Evening Post* to contemplate the works of Van Dyck and Rembrandt . . .